EB & FLOW

Also by Kelly J. Baptist

EB & FLOW

KELLY J. BAPTIST

Crown Books for Young Readers
New York

Text copyright © 2023 by Kelly J. Baptist
Jacket art copyright © 2023 by Shannon Wright

Visit us on the Web! rhcbooks.com

Educators and librarians, for a variety of teaching tools, visit us at
RHTeachersLibrarians.com

Library of Congress Cataloging-in-Publication Data is available upon request.
ISBN 978-0-593-42913-6 (hardcover) — ISBN 978-0-593-42914-3 (lib. bdg.) —
ISBN 978-0-593-42915-0 (ebook)

The text of this book is set in 12-point Archer Book.
Interior design by Cathy Bobak

Printed in the United States of America
10 9 8 7 6 5 4 3 2 1
First Edition

Random House Children's Books supports the First Amendment
and celebrates the right to read.

For Dameon, MarKayla, and Treyjen. Thank you for inspiring me. Each of you has enough light to inspire THE WORLD! I can't wait to see it!

THE DAY OF

FLOW

I don't hit girls.
I don't even hit girls ... is what I'm thinking
but I musta said it out loud because Mr. Warren,
our bald-headed principal, raises his eyebrows and says,
"You sure about that? Our cameras
show us something very different, De'Kari."

"It's Flow," I say. I *always* say it.

"Your name is De'Kari Flood, and that's
what I'm calling you," says Mr. Warren.

Just like everyone else.

I roll my eyes, turn them to my shoes.

New shoes.
Shoes I'ma wear every day till they fall off my feet.

EB

"He called me the b-word.

And it was all just an accident!
Nobody was trying to mess up
his Stupid Ugly Shoes."

My arms are crossed, and I'm giving Mr. Warren
the same look I seen Ma give my sister, Poke,
when Poke comes at her wrong.

Ma learned The Look from my granny,
who be givin' it to all of us when we're wrong.
I'm not tryna be no poet, but
        Poke ain't no Joke.
So she gets The Look a lot.
Guess I do, too.

Few more minutes of this with Mr. Warren,
and then my granny will be on the phone
listening to him tell her
allllllll about
how
        Ebony
            got to fighting
again.

"So you stepped on his shoes by accident?"

"YES!"

Sometimes I be thinkin' Mr. Warren
can't hear that good.
He asks the same questions
    over
       and over.

"And then he called you a name?"

"The b-word."

Get it right, Mr. Warren.

"And then?"

"I slapped him in his ugly face."

Yeah. I slapped him good, too!
Everybody in the lunchroom went,
     "OOOOOOOH!"

"Then he pushed you?" Mr. Warren asks,
lookin' all concerned.

"And I pushed him back!" I say.
    Loud.
"You seen the video—why you wastin' time asking?"

Mr. Warren ignores my question.
He good at that.

"What happened after you pushed him?"

I let the question
    hang.

I glue my hand to my leg to keep from touching
        my left cheek, which throbs.
If I wasn't dark like Milky Way Midnights,
        I'd be red right there.
Like that cinnamon gum Poke's boyfriend loves.

Because that can't-rap fool, who calls himself Flow,

swung
on
me.

FLOW

Mr. Warren's the mean principal.
The one giving suspensions out like M&M's
and making kids go to detention and stuff.

Mr. Porter's the nice principal who talks
at assemblies and can actually dance.

If you're student of the week, he buys you lunch,
    whatever you want.
And if you get on
"Principal Porter's list,"
there's a fancy banquet.

        I ain't on
        nobody's list,
        and I don't care.

Except ... Mr. Warren pulls up my grades,
tells me I'm close.

    Close to having them add my name to a list
    but which one
        is up
    to me.

EB

Third suspension of seventh grade.
    Eighth since I been at Brookside Junior High.
Mr. Warren tells me this like I don't know.

It's a lot.
    So?

Maybe if people stop messin' with me ...

"Did you apologize?"

    "Huh?"

"You said it was an accident," Mr. Warren says.

He leans forward. "Did you apologize to De'Kari
for stepping on his shoes?"

"Yeah," I say,
    rolling my eyes ... and the lie.

FLOW

"How come you didn't get an adult?"

They always ask this.

C'mon, man. You got "war" in your name.
Don't act like
You
    Don't
        Know.

That's what my shrug says.

"Look at me," Mr. Warren says.
"Real men look eye to eye."

I glare at him. Silent.
Oh yeah?

A real man also don't get punked by no stupid girl.
I got scratches on the side of my face from that girl!

"Y'all gotta learn how to let stuff go."

My brain screams,

That's the problem, Mr. Warren!

Everything I have,
    everything I love

    already goes.

EB

I shift in the seat, and my back shouts.

My face must show it.

"Are you okay?" asks Mr. Warren.

I only nod.

But I already know this really gonna hurt tomorrow,
just like when I fought Shaya.

I barely remember what happened
   after I pushed De'Kari . . .
        after he socked me.

I heard kids sayin',

"OOOOH, he slammed her!" after they broke us up
        and dragged us to the guidance office.

Great.

I bet Jonetta and Bri and them were recording
   on their phones.
They do that with all the fights.

I suck my teeth, sigh.

Mr. Warren sighs, too.

"Are we calling your grandmother?"

Mr. Warren dials. "I hope these ten days give you plenty of time to think about the path you're on, Ebony."

Whatever.

Granny picks up and Mr. Warren puts
   on his principal voice.

"Good afternoon, Mrs. Lewis. This is Principal Warren at Brookside—"

"Ah naw! Do NOT tell me Ebony in trouble *again*?"

I wince when I hear her voice.

Mr. Warren explains the fight, what he *think* happened. Tells Granny I got ten days.

   "Put her on the phone," Granny demands.

I groan when Mr. Warren puts it on speaker.

"Granny, I ain't even do nothing!" I start.

"Betta shut that mouth! I'm 'bout sick of getting calls from that school!"

"But he—"

Doesn't matter what I say. Granny barrels over
   my words.
"Poke got the car; can't get you till she's off work."

"That's alright," Mr. Warren says. "She'll finish the day in the Focus Center."

No one listens when I say that's the last place
on earth I wanna be.

FLOW

I didn't call her the b-word.

Even if he don't believe me, I still need to say it.

It was probably Greg. He calls all the girls that word.
    I'm not about to snitch, cuz it don't even matter now
and that's not what we do.

But Mr. Warren needs to know.

EB

Poke works at Rainbow, the one in the same plaza
as Target and PetSmart.
She lucky to have that job, 'specially after our cousin
Ty'ree stole some stuff from there.
    Tried to, anyway.
Ladies' boots with fur inside, an off-brand jersey,
And a wallet.
Dumb stuff.
He got caught quick.
Poke says the smartest thing he did was
act like he didn't know her.

That was a few years ago, but Granny still don't like
when I tease him and say,

"Ty'ree rhymes with *free!*"

Ty'ree the kind of cousin you glad is your cousin,
    blood cousin,
and not
your enemy.

FLOW

I already know what's gonna happen before
Mr. Warren picks up the phone:

Call Ma first.
    No answer.
She's at work, cell phone off.
Next up, my dad.
But ten digits won't get Dad's voice.

Not no more.

"Who's Reggie Springer?"

My heart starts pounding.
Ma put *him* down as a contact?

"Just call my brother, Cas," I say.

But nah, Mr. Warren gotta be difficult
and call my uncle Reggie anyway.

I'm prayin' prayin' prayin' . . . that Uncle Reggie's busy
changing oil, rotating tires, fixin' engines,
so he can't get the phone.

Prayer must work, at least for now.

Mr. Warren gotta dial the numbers I give him.
My big bro picks up right away,
and he says those magic words:

He coming to get me.

EB

The Focus Center is a joke when Mr. Ford is in there
and like a prison when it's Ms. Humphries.

   "Eyes ahead, no talking!" Ms. Humphries says
   as soon as I slump into my seat.

I'm sitting behind Big Mike, so hopefully she won't see
   me when I slide my phone from my pocket
   and text Poke,

BEG her to come get me.

Seven other kids in here, all doing boring worksheets.
I'm sure Ms. Humphries balls them up
and trashes them when we leave.

It's quiet, but the stares are loud.
They all talking with their eyes.
That's the one . . .
the one that smacked that boy.
In the lunchroom?
    Yeah.
I heard he bodied her!
    He prolly did!
      That's what she get!

I narrow my eyes, but soon it makes my cheek hurt.
My nose hurts, too.
I check my phone again.
Missed texts.
Angie, askin' if I'm aight.
Kianna, sayin' De'Kari was wrong for what he did.
Precious, tellin' me it's on Snapchat and IG.

I'm gonna send Poke ten million texts
till she leaves Rainbow and comes here.
I keep looking out the window for her car.
But all I see is De'Kari and some older guy.
They prolly laughing.
De'Kari's brother or cousin or whatever
prolly proud, sayin', "Good job, bro!

You put that b in her place!"

I hate the prickly way tears feel
when your eyes don't want them to come.

It burns until you blink and blink.

Poke. Doesn't. Text. Me. Back.

FLOW

"What was yo' dumb self thinkin'?" goes Cas.

His words hit me, same as the cold air,
when we get outside.

"You hittin' girls now?"
Cas punches my shoulder.

"Nah, it wasn't like that," I try to explain. "She—"

"You can chill with all that," Cas cuts me off. "Ma gonna
lose it. *Ten* days, bro?"

Man.
I slam the car door when I climb inside.
Cas gives me a warning look, so I stare out the window.

Brookside speeds by as Cas drives.

Gray. Bumpy.
Familiar, like a favorite hoodie . . .
Nothing brand new.

People say it's a town you don't wanna leave,
and even if you do, you always come back.

They also say it's a town you *wanna* leave but don't.

People say Brookside is a bad place.

Scary.

But we got Mr. Crenshaw, who barbecues in
   super-short shorts and boots, no matter how hot or cold,
and if we walk by his house while he's out there,
he *always* slides us a wing or drumstick.
Miz Turner hands out Band-Aids if somebody gets hurt.
If you into ball, Money Mack helps us kids
   get our game right.

And we got Larry's, the BEST burger place in the world.

So people need to know.

        Where I live is more than just one thing.

EB

Granny's lips are pressed tight,
   and she's gripping her purse
like a football she can't fumble.
It was mad awkward when they called my name
on the intercom.

"Excuse the interruption, staff and students.
   Ebony Wilson to the main office with her belongings
   to go."

Everybody looked at me. . . .
Probably all thinking . . .

Yup, she's suspended.

Granny has Jaren with her.
      He my nephew, Poke's baby.
He's two, but nowhere near terrible.
He smiles when he sees me and runs over.
I can't help smilin', too, cuz of how cute he is.
Plus, his is probably the only smile
I'ma get today.

FLOW

My brother's name is David, but everybody calls him Cas,
short for Casper, as in Casper the Friendly Ghost.
Cas's dad says when Cas was born, he was so bright
EVERYBODY was side-eyein' my mama.

His dad called him Casper and then just Cas,
and then it stuck.

My dad did the same thing with me.
He took videos on his phone of when I was a baby

doing that cute baby-talk stuff.

He said, "Listen to him go! This kid got flow!"

And he started calling me that.

Flow.

But I don't got flow like him. (He was pretty well-known
for his rhymes.)

I got flow like me. (I'm not well-known, but I'm a beast
in the water.)

And unlike Cas, my nickname didn't stick with Ma.

Just with my dad.

DAY ONE

EB

First day of suspension . . .
first thing Granny snatches is my phone,
which ain't no big surprise.

    "You just got off Christmas break,
and this what you do?"

She keep sayin' the same thing, but
  she don't ask about my back.
And if she notices the puffiness on my cheek,
  she don't say nothing.

Today she makes me watch Jaren
  so she can run errands alone.

Fine by me.

He just needs Cheerios and *PJ Masks* and he good to go.

I log on to my school account from
   the computer in the TV room,
open a Google Doc, and share it with Kianna,
like we always do when one of us is suspended.

I type
      she got my phone of course.
And a few minutes later, Kianna logs in to the doc.
She's in social studies with Ms. Henry.
Kianna hates that class, and I
low-key love it,
low-key hate that I'm missing it.
Kianna types
      that sucks, school's boring.
      Angie said, De'Kari said something about you on
         IG.
I type
      Wat he say?

Takes Kianna a few minutes.
Ms. Henry must be walkin' around,
   checkin' Chromebooks.
She do that a lot.
      IDK, she said somebody told her he was talkin'
         mess.
            Gotta go!
Kianna's dolphin profile pic disappears
   before I can say bye.

FLOW

I guess sleeping in ain't gonna happen.

My uncle Reggie flicks my room light on at 5:30 a.m.
An hour before I usually get up for school.

"You like to fight, big man?"
Big man is not *Flow*, so I fake like I'm still asleep.

"Boy, get up!"

Suddenly my blanket's in Uncle Reggie's bear paw and
I'm instantly cold.

"You wanna be a fighter, you should train like one."
Uncle Reggie has on sweatpants and a pissed-off scowl.

Bad combo.

"Nah, brooooo," I groan.

"Your 'bro' is probably still bundled up in his
    big-boy blanket on somebody's funky couch,
    which, I guess, is better than a jail cot,
which is what you'll be sleeping on if you keep
    fighting at school."

I get up.

Sit-ups. Push-ups. Jumping jacks.

I glare at Uncle Reggie the whole time,
    but he just evil-laughs,

says, "Fix ya face, Ali!"
Toxic.

Ma don't even save me when she gets up at 6:15.
She barely looks at me on her way out when she says,
"No gaming" and "I'm going up to school for your work."
Without her usual goodbye kiss that I count on.

To tell the truth, I'm too exhausted to even think
        about gaming or homework.
All I want is my bed.

EB

Jaren got a whole bunch of energy!
He do this thing where he runs top speed at the couch
and slams into the cushions and bounces onto the
    floor,
laughing
        laughing
            laughing
like it's the funniest thing in the world.

"BeeBee!" he squeals, trying to get me to do it, too.

That's what he call me, BeeBee.
Not *auntie*, not *TT*, not Ebony or Eb.
    BeeBee.

I tell this li'l boy I ain't runnin' into no couch,
   but he's so, so cute
and his chubby, warm hand keeps grabbing mine and
   pullin' with no power at all,
so *finally* I get up from the computer
and fake-run with him into the couch.
We both gigglin' and lookin' mad silly.
I bet if I could take Jaren to school with me,
I'd be laughin' too much to ever be fighting.

FLOW

I'm starving when I wake up again.
Lucky for me there's some greens and corn bread
and sweet potatoes left over from Sunday.
I warm it up and demolish it.
The best thing about Uncle Reggie is that he can cook.
The worst thing is that he owns a garage three blocks away
and can pop up anytime.

Like now.

His truck rumbles into the driveway, and I barely
have time to move before he busts into the kitchen.

"No plate for me, nephew?" he goes,

and I almost choke on a hunk of corn bread.
Corn bread be doin' that, if you breathe wrong while
   eating it.

Uncle Reggie pours himself a glass of orange juice,
watches me.
He's in his blue AutoKings jumpsuit, and I feel kinda
    dumb in my T-shirt and boxers.

"It's slow right now," Uncle Reggie says. "Get dressed."

I open my mouth, start to complain, but his glass
    hits the counter
pretty hard and he points at me.

"Nah. We ain't even doin' all that."

Uncle Reggie opens the door to go outside.

"Ten minutes."

I slam my plate in the sink, say words to the air
that I can't say to him.
Pull on a hoodie and jeans too big, but Cas
gave 'em to me, so I make it work.
Reach for my shoes, the ones my dad
gave me on Christmas three weeks ago.
I want to put them on cuz I said I would wear them
every
single
day
till they fall apart.
But that barbecue sauce splash is still on the toe

of the left one, and the scuff marks are black gashes
on the right one.

"You did all that over some damn shoes?" Ma had yelled
when she got home from work and read
   the suspension letter.
My brain went blank, mouth went frozen, too, and I
   couldn't tell her
they aren't
just
shoes.

I wear my boots instead.

EB

Granny lives in one of those houses on Grand Avenue.
It's big but old.
Real nice back then, back when they first bought it.
It needs work, lots of work, to make it look how it does
in the pictures in Granny's photo albums.

When we used to come over, for visits, not to live,
us kids would always be grabbing those photo albums to
   look at all those old pictures
   where everything looked brand new.

Granny would say, "Brookside was the place to be
in those days, and Grand Avenue was just like its name."

Granny's house has more rooms than ours did.
She say those rooms held all her children . . . but she
    ain't expect them to
have to hold her grandchildren and great-grandchildren,
    too.

Upstairs, my little sister, Aubrey, and me share a room.
Poke got a room with Jaren, but now that he's two,
she been putting him in with Courtney, my little brother.
When he ain't in trouble, my cousin Ty'ree
got a room here, too.
His is the smallest.
Us kids gotta share the bathroom up here.

Downstairs is Granny's room, door always closed, but
I remember playing in her closet and trying on her wigs.
Then there's Granny's sewing room, which she also don't
    like us going in, even though she barely goes in there
    anymore.
Then there's Granny's bathroom. Kitchen.
"Sitting" room, now TV room (cuz of all us kids).

The room that's been mine for a year used to be
Mama's for eighteen.
I loved sleeping in here for visits.
I hate sleeping in here for living.
It don't make no sense that we here in her room
and she stays ten minutes

away.

FLOW

Brookside High School. BHS. Home of the Panthers.

Place where Uncle Reggie got the ladies
and fought the fellas.

Place where my mom first holla'd at my dad after he
rapped at the talent show their sophomore year.
(He didn't holla back for a decade, but it's cool. . . .)

Place where Cas was a state champion in track
and football and almost basketball . . .
that buzzer beater had him depressed for days.

Place where Black and Gold mean everything.
Place where you gotta be tough, no matter what.

Place where there's no pool for swimming.

Place where I don't wanna go even though Ma did and

my dad and Cas and
everybody.

Place we pass on the way to the garage,
and unlike Uncle Reggie,
who grins, points, and goes, "Yooo, BROOKSIDE!"

I feel
lost.

The only school with an indoor pool
is across the bridge in Manchester Heights.
St. Vincent's.

EB

My face look worse today.
When they say black 'n' blue, it's true.
I'm glad for these ten days; it would suck to have to
go to school looking like this.
Granny finally notices: "That boy did that?"
I'm on the couch with Jaren halfway on my lap.
We been chillin' with this show for a good minute.
I glance at Granny and nod.
Her face is a frown.

"Now that's a shame."

Part of me wants her to go after him,
to call up his mama and cuss her out:
> Make sure your blankity-blank son keeps his
>> blankity-blank hands
> off
> my granddaughter!

I can't see Granny doing that, though.

Mama?
Yes.

If she:
   knew.
   cared.
   was here.

Granny asks, "Why you wanna fight with boys, Eb?"

"I didn't even do nothin' to him, Granny!" I say.
But I gotta keep my eyes on the TV screen when I say it.

"They say you messed up the boy's shoes;
slapped him dead in the face!"

"Look at *my* face, Granny!"

    She does.

    That same part of me wants her to just hug me.

"My back hurts, too."
    Granny's face is concerned.

"Can I take a bath in your tub?"

Granny loves her baths, and her tub is always clean,
Unlike the one us kids gotta share.

Granny might be mad at me, but she ain't gonna say no
  if I'm hurt.
Which I am.

I keep the water on till she yells about the bill.
I pour in lavender bodywash to get bubbles,
  and when I climb in,
I'm doing everything to forget about the fight, but it
  sticks to me like
black
and
blue.

FLOW

It's freezing cold in Uncle Reggie's shop.
Don't know how he stands it.

"Pete, Magic, y'all remember this li'l knucklehead."

Magic goes, "Li'l Flow, whatcha know?"
I give him dap.

"Ain't you 'pose to be in school?" Pete asks.

"Got suspended," I mumble.
        "What they get you for?" asks Magic.
"Fighting."

The guys hoot.

"That's how come you got them scratches
    on yo' face, huh?
        How the other guy look?"

"You mean, other girl?" Uncle Reggie says.
"This fool was fighting a female."

And then it gets quiet.

"Nah, we cain't have that," says Pete, his smile gone.

"My thoughts exactly," says Uncle Reggie.

I get it.
He's tryna teach me a lesson, use his boys to help him.

"Got his fists balled up like he wanna fight right now,"
    Pete says.

Instigator.

At school, we can get in trouble for being one of those.

I make my face blank, cold like the temp,
    and look past them . . .
to the ugly car with its hood up, all its business out there
for everybody to see and talk about. . . .

Like mine is.

Uncle Reggie starts to say something else,
    but then the door to the waiting area opens
    and a guy in a camouflage coat and
    matching Timbs comes in.

"Ahh, right on time!" Uncle Reggie says.

"No doubt," the dude replies, giving Uncle Reggie a nod.

He looks like he's Cas's age, maybe older.
Uncle Reggie introduces him around,
    the new oil-change guy.
Pete takes him, and Magic takes me.
But I don't want to see a cracked radiator
    or a worn-out tire.
This ain't gonna be what I do.
The name "Flow" don't match with mechanic.

It matches with:
    water.
    movement.
    smooth.

EB

I love Kianna and all but she low-key kinda fake.
I'm on the Google Doc, waiting.
I know she in study skills, boring last class of the day,
and I *know* she messin' around on her Chromebook
instead of doing homework like she supposed to.
So why ain't she in the doc?
I send an email:

    Yo Kianna, did you check IG? Wat he say?
I gotta keep watching for Granny, who keep watching
    my screen whenever she walks by.
I click over to Newsela, read the article
  about coins in the US,
which is actually kinda interesting.
I answer the questions before checking my email again.

Nothing.

C'mon, Kianna! She trippin'.

I do a few math worksheets, cuz Granny
  wouldn't leave the school yesterday
    until they gave me a ton of work to take home.

The Distributive Property of Ebony says that

Me times Never-Ending Homework

Plus

Me times a Ten-Day Suspension

Equals

The Worst
Answer
Ever.

FLOW

The garage gets busy around two, so Uncle Reggie
lets me walk home.
"Betta get right there," he warns.
And I do ... after stopping by the gas station
for some snacks.
I'm grabbing Hot Fries and Sour Patch Kids and 7UP
when somebody calls out to me.
        "Yo, De'Kari!"
I look over my shoulder.
Bryce Pearson.
His brother, Brandon, right behind him,
    and his boy Jay-Jay
trailin' both of them.

"Sup," I say.
"Y'all suspended, too?"

"Nah, bro." Jay-Jay grins.

I'm not shocked.
These three love to skip last hour.
Call themselves the Three Kings.
Mrs. Harrison, who tries to get kids
   to play chess at school,
says they're more like three pawns.

"Yo, you *bodied* Ebony, bro!" Bryce laughs.

I feel kinda sick.
"You saw the video?"

"Nah."
I grab my snacks, move to leave.

"Her homegirls runnin' they mouths now," Jay-Jay says.
His words hold me when I want to just keep walking.
"They sayin' she gonna get her cousin to handle you
      or something."

"Man, whatever," I say.
"I got a big brother; cousins, too!"
But my chest tightens a little
   after what Brandon says next.

"I hear he an Ace."

That floats in the air a minute.

Heavy.

Then Bryce goes,

"So? De'Kari gon' have the Three Kings ridin' for him
if stuff goes down."

Sounds good and all, but we know Three Kings ain't
  Aces.

"Flow," I say.

Huh? is written all over their faces.
"Oh yeah," says Bryce. "I forgot you go by that."

"So you gonna be a rapper?" Brandon asks.

"Y'all hurry up; you can chitchat outside!"
  the cashier guy interrupts.

He's always trippin' 'bout kids being in the store,
but I guess it's cuz kids always be stealin'.

"Y'all should be in school anyway," the guy keeps on.

Brandon makes a face, mouths off,
  "Maybe you should be, too!
Working in this broke-down gas station!"

"Take your smart mouth outta here!" the guy yells.

Bryce tells him to shut up, to not talk to his brother.
He's protective like that.

The guy says,
nah,
nah,
he don't gotta shut up cuz a kid said so,
    and while they're going
back
        and
forth,
Jay-Jay's snatchin' stuff like he don't know they got
    cameras everywhere just waiting for somebody
    to push play and rewind and zoom
and see Skittles and Starburst and Paydays in pockets.

Cas told me 'bout those cameras.

I put down the 7UP and the Hot Fries
and the Sour Patches and I bounce.

Walking home is different from walking here cuz I'm
    watching over my shoulder,
    thinking every dude I see could be
Ebony's cousin, the Ace.

EB

Ty'ree say he got a job, so Granny let him
stay in his room again.
I like when Ty'ree is here.

Not as much as Courtney does, though.
Courtney's seven, and he pretends Ty'ree is his
   big brother
since we don't have one.
Courtney gets this hyena laugh when Ty'ree picks him up
and tickles him.
Then Aubrey gets jealous, and Ty'ree has to pick her up, too.
When they catch me watching, Ty'ree says,
   "Whatchoo over there lookin' at?" and I try
   but I can't hide my smile and I can't stop my laugh
when Ty'ree grabs me, too.

But later, Ty'ree gets serious, says,

"I don't like that a boy put his hands on you."

Granny's helping Aubrey and Courtney with homework,
so it's just me and Ty'ree.

"Who is he?"

I shrug. Look away. "Just some stupid boy."

Ty'ree frowns. His tank top lets me study
   the tattoos on his right arm,
like they're a map from geography class.
The map of Ty'ree.
A skull, an ace of spades card, a racetrack,
his best friend's name with dates,
our cousin Mookie's name with dates,

something from the Bible,
a fist.

"All I know is, it bet'not happen again," Ty'ree tells me.
"You just tell me who it is, and I'll take care of it."

He gets up, prolly to fix another plate or get a root beer.
Ty'ree eats like that, nonstop.
I'm supposed to be doing quiet reading, but now
  all I hear is
    Ty'ree's words.

When I brush my teeth.
When I'm in the shower.
When I'm in the bed, listening to Aubrey snore,

I'll take care of it
take care of it
take care
of it.

And that's exactly what De'Kari deserves.

DAY TWO

EB

Poke shakes me hard to wake me up.
"Come downstairs and watch Jaren."

I groan, try to hide under covers. "Where Granny at?"
I ask, even though I know what she gonna say now.

"Don't worry 'bout where she at!
   If your butt was in school,
we wouldn't be having this conversation!"

That's been their answer for everything.

If your butt was in school ...

I slide out of bed, make sure Poke know
   I ain't down with this.
"Stop gettin' suspended, then," she tells me.
She lookin' kinda bummy: sweatpants, jacket, and boots.
   "Where you goin'?" I demand.

"Nunya."

Ugh. Attitude.
That's how Poke got her name anyway.
Lips was always poked out for miles, and everybody
  forgot about Serenity,
her real name, and started calling her Poke,
  which really fits.

I find Jaren at the table with pancake pieces
  and a syrupy smile.

"BeeBee, wook!" he say, showing me his bacon.

There ain't no plate for me.

"It's bacon. So what," I tell him.

"Uh-uh, don't be all funky to my baby," Poke tells me.

"Then take your baby with you!" I suggest.

"You and that mouth," Poke says.
  "I see why you stay fightin'."

Poke leaves before I can say the mouth I got
  is the same one she got.
The one WE got from our mama.

FLOW

I got a little sister, Myesha.
She's seven, and I bet if she ever got suspended,

Uncle Reggie wouldn't have her up at 5:30 a.m.
    doing jumping jacks
and running in place.

Myesha asks me why I ain't in school.

"Myesha, man, mind yo' business," I say.
She get mad, tells Ma I snapped at her, and of course,

Ma goes *all* the way off.

"Why can't she ask you? If you ashamed,
    you shouldn't've acted the fool!
If your butt was at school, she wouldn't have to ask!"

So I tell Myesha I got suspended and she goes,
"Oooooh! You a bad kid?"
Ma lookin' at me like, *Yeah, tell her.*
I don't got much to say, other than "Naw,"
cuz I'm not a bad kid.
Not really.
Not at all.

EB

Jaren wants to play with Legos, but I don't.
So I bring his tub of bricks downstairs
    so I can get on the computer
and share a doc with Kianna.

Even though I know she's in language arts, where I
    would be right now,
and she should have her Chromebook,
I never see the dolphin pic log in to the doc.
I try Angie,
        type, **hey girl**
and wait. . . .
After a few minutes, she logs in to the doc.

        OMG Eb, you okay?
Yeah.
        **De'Kari's dumb friends talkin' 'bout how he mad
        you got him suspended.**
So?
        **They was talkin' 'bout going to your house and
        doing something. Just watch yo' back, aight?**

Angie types other stuff, stupid stuff, like how C.J.
    already said he going to the Valentine's dance with
    Kianna and how Kianna thinks Trey is gonna
    ask her, too, and how Mr. Long farted in class
    and got mad when kids was laughin'.

There's not much for me to type back.

I'm watchin' my li'l nephew.
I'm the new dishwasher of the family.
I'm gettin' side-eyed by Granny.
I'm wonderin' if De'Kari really gonna try something.

When Angie has to go, I turn off the computer without
   doing any work and build a spaceship for Jaren.

FLOW

Ma really loved her new job
        at first.
I think it's
a little different
        now.
She's the office manager
for CareNow,
where you go if you sick
or sprained your ankle
or got pink eye
and don't wanna wait
three hours
at the hospital.
Ma says
that *manager* means
if a receptionist calls off
or a nurse takes vacation,
she either has to figure it out
or do their job.
She comes home stressed,
sighs a lot,
rubs her forehead,

tells stories of patients being
rude,
unintelligent,
ignorant.
Sometimes we laugh
at those stories.
Sometimes we stay quiet
while Ma vents.
Sometimes Ma falls asleep
with her work clothes on.

Me and Myesha
sometimes tell her
to just take
a day off.

Ma always
says
no.

EB

I guess
Legos ain't so bad.
I'm building stuff
longer than Jaren,
who starts whining
that he hungry . . .

again.
I fix peanut butter and jelly
and keep
building
my tower.
Who knew
the clicking sound
of Legos snapping together
is
so
cool.

Or that
I can make something
out of pieces . . .
annoying pieces
that sometimes get
stepped on,
cussed at,
lost,
thrown away.

"Ohhhh noooo!"
Jaren yells
when his tower
falls apart.
"It bwoken, BeeBee!"

"Naw, it's not," I tell him.

"Lego pieces always fit."

I snap
a few
together
and BOOM!

"See?"

Not broken anymore.

FLOW

After I wake up (for the second time)
I just lay in the bed
and listen to the quiet house.
Three bedrooms, two bathrooms,
   basement that nobody really goes in
   except Uncle Reggie,
   and now me, cuz he got me
   doing these stupid early-morning workouts . . .
garage, small backyard with a grill and a fence. . . .

Our house is the only house I know.
   Definitely don't remember the apartment we stayed at
   when I was just a baby.
But our house is a different house with Daddy

not here.

EB

Granny drops an orange folder on the floor next to me.
She was a teacher for, like, forty years or something
so she don't play when it comes to school stuff.

"This ain't no vacation," she say. "You had your vacation.
Christmas is over."

I open the folder.

Worksheets.
Millions of them, from all my teachers.
I know better than to groan and complain
    and suck my teeth.
The look on Granny's face almost dares me
    to do any of that.
"C'mon," she say, and I follow her to the kitchen,
where I fill in maps of Africa, do math problems with
    X's and O's,
and read boring paragraphs with
    endless dumb questions

while Granny fries chicken cuz she's in the mood to.
I get real mad when I imagine De'Kari/Wannabe Flow.
He probably chillin', gaming, and doing whatever else
stupid boys do.
And I'm stuck with all this work.

FLOW

Uncle Reggie comes at noon, stack of papers in his hand.
So glad I didn't have the PlayStation on yet.

"Went to your school. Your mama don't want you
falling behind."

I take the stack, make a face.
They're a little stained with car grease.

"We ain't really talked about it," Uncle Reggie says.

He means the fight.

"Now I know you gonna be gettin' into scuffles
here and there, but when it comes to young ladies . . ."

Uncle Reggie pauses.

My chest tightens. I know what he wants to say

but won't say.

Can't say.

Instead he points to the papers before he leaves.

"Put in work on those."

EB

Watermelon Jolly Ranchers are my favorite.
So when I remember I got a pack in my book bag,
the day gets better.

I dump all the flavors on the floor. Six cherries,
    four sour apples, seven blue raspberries,
    and only three watermelons.
It's 'bout to be zero.

"Wan' some!" goes Jaren, banging into my room
and seeing my stash. I almost *almost* yell at him
    to get out,
leave me alone, but he'll cry, and Granny will start
    fussin', asking if
I hit him or something.

So two blue raspberries and one sour apple
keep him quiet for a minute.

Not long enough.

Jaren points at my face. "Owwee?" he asks
again and again, till I say,

"Yes! Damn!"

Then he grins, repeats what I said
again
and
again.

"No, no, no, don't say that!" I tell him.

But he still goes, "Owwee, yes, damn!" when he leaves
    my room.

FLOW

Look,

it ain't go down like how everybody thinks.
Ma's mad cuz she thinks people think
I ain't got home-training.
She say she ain't raise me to hit girls.
Thing is,

I KNOW!

She thinks I'm gonna be like him . . .

My dad.

Which is cool with me.

Except for the time my dad

hit

Ma.

EB

Granny don't usually get this mad.

She got it all wrong. I ain't teachin' Jaren to cuss.
That's NOT what happened!

"It slipped out!" I say. "He was buggin' me!"

But that don't stop fire from shooting out of
    Granny's eyes.
She narrows them and takes aim at me.

"See! I'm too old for this!
You don't stop causing me grief!
I do yo' mama a favor, and this is the thanks I get!
Get her on the phone; you can go stay with her!"

Once Granny's outta bullets, she sends me to my room.

I don't even have my phone to call Mama,
but if I did, what she gon' say?

Do better, Eb! Stop stressin' your granny out!
You just like yo' daddy!
But it's never

Eb, how 'bout you come here with me.

FLOW

I was five.

They was fighting, screaming, cussing.

Mad.

Ma threw something at my dad. But not just anything . . .
    a glass vase.

But not just any vase . . . a glass vase his mom, my nana,
    had given him
when she was alive.

I remember that vase. It was clear, but Cas and me swore
    it changed colors,
blue, green, and yellow when you put flowers in it.
Nana's vase is what my dad called it.

Ma threw Nana's vase,
my dad ducked,
and it shattered on the floor.

I remember both sounds.

The glass breaking and the
THWUNK
of Dad's hand on Ma's cheek.

And then, no sounds but tears and
*sorry*s.

He only did it once . . . that time Ma broke Nana's vase.

And now Ma probably thinks I'm him. Just like him.

I wanna tell her,

Okay, then. I messed up.

But if I'm just like him, I only did it once.

EB

I could walk to Mama's house if I wanted to.
If it wasn't so freakin' cold out and I had my phone
and earbuds, some hot Cheetos, and a Cherry 7UP,
I would do it.

Me, Aubrey, and Courtney did it once.
    Walked.
We was playing outside Granny's house and Courtney goes,
"I wanna see Mama."

"I know where she live at!" Aubrey said.

"So?" I told both of them. "Everybody know where she stay."

1771 Morton.

We lived a bunch of places:
    Parker Homes, Apartment 3C.
    902 N. Center Road.
    River Trace Apartments, #627.
And with Granny, 2408 Grand Avenue.

But we never lived at 1771 Morton.

When we walked over that time, we was sweaty and thirsty
and happy that we made it, finally.
And it was a cute li'l house, too.

    "That's my window!" Courtney yelled.

"That's mine!" Aubrey pointed.

I was just about to pick my window when Mama opened
the front door and stepped onto the porch.
Her face was a giant *"What the??!!"* and she said,
"How y'all get here?"

We walked, Mama. We walked for almost an hour
to see you.

And it only took fifteen minutes for her to drive us back.

DAY THREE

FLOW

Uncle Reggie's yawning
   during jumping jacks and sit-ups today,
so I'm betting he gonna let this go soon.

EB

It's finally quiet when I wake up.

I know I'm not supposed to, but since Poke took
   Jaren to a doctor's appointment,
I figure I got a few hours to chill
in front of the TV.

Granny say I gotta sweep *and* mop all the floors,
but she can miss me with all that.

It's like I'm their little maid just cuz I'm suspended.

   Clean this, clean that, watch Jaren . . .

I'm sick of it!

I watch *Real Live Basketball Wives* and imagine
   I'm rich enough
to have petty drama and still look cute.

Trey Karson, this boy at my school, plays ball.
He's good . . .
all the girls be going on and on 'bout how fine he is.

In the lunchroom that day, Kianna had dared me
   to go over and see
who he asking to the Valentine's dance in a few weeks.

She wanted me to ask for her . . .
   but as I walked over I knew
I was gonna be askin' for me
cuz deep down
for real for real
I knew Trey liked me.

So I was thinkin' hard 'bout how Kianna gonna take that,
and I didn't see Paris running from silly-butt Randy.
She almost slammed into me, so I moved out the way
fast
and tripped
on De'Kari's

shoes.

FLOW

I don't think I'm gonna be a rapper like my dad was.
I'm a different kinda Flow, but don't nobody know.
I feel calm and peaceful and just left alone when I'm
in water.

    Yup, water.

I don't know nobody else who likes to swim.
Ma be sayin', "Black folks don't go in the water
  like that."

She's wrong.

Cuz I do. And today, I think I'm gonna walk
  to the rec center

and swim.

EB

Yesterday Granny made us get up early for church,
  which was really messed up cuz normally
we go to second service.

When I tried to remind her, she snapped on me.
"Girl, you of all people need Jesus all day!"
And then she made us stay for both services!

Poke was lucky; she had to work.

Ty'ree tried to lie and say he had work, too,
but Granny shut that down quick. "You tryna
play a playa, huh?" she said.
"That garage ain't open today!
And if you livin' in MY house,
you go where I say,
when *I* say!"

I got scared when she said that
   cuz I didn't want Ty'ree to leave
like he always do when she says mess like that.

This time, though, he didn't. He got up, took a shower,
and put on a nice shirt and khakis that hung low on him,
but not so low for Granny to start fussin'.

Everybody was showin' Granny love at church,
acting like she was a hero for makin' all of us come.
We filled a whole row—

me, Granny, Jaren, Aubrey, Courtney, and Ty'ree.

Not gon' lie, it was nice to get out the house
even if it was just for church.

FLOW

Pretty sure Ma only let me keep my cell so she can
boss me around from work.

Take the trash out—all the trash!

Make sure you wash the dishes—all the dishes!

I want five pages of that homework done!

She been textin' me since 8:00 a.m.!
    And I know if I ignore them,
she'll send Uncle Reggie, which I do
NOT
want.

Ma ain't the only one texting me, though.

Ebony's ugly-butt friends added me to a group chat,
and ain't nothin' pretty about what they sayin'.

They sayin' I posted a video of the fight, which I didn't,
and that I'm braggin' to neighborhood dudes,
    which I'm not.

They go in with the name-callin' and say what they
and everybody else gonna do to me.

So, what I'm supposed to do but type
    some heat of my own,
push Send.

And we go back and forth like Ping-Pong till I'm mad . . .

Mad at that stupid girl who stepped on my shoes.

My NEW shoes.

On purpose.

Her and her stupid friends all deserve to get hit.

EB

Jaren's crying when he comes home with Poke,
   so I guess he got shots or something.
    His face is lookin' mad busted,
all tears and snot, and he got a toy in his hand,
   like they tried to
Happy Meal it all away.

     Big fail . . .

But when Jaren sees me, he runs top speed to me
and buries his nasty snot-'n'-tear face
   in my favorite hoodie.

I'm two seconds from yelling at him
   but he holds me so tight
and it hits me that Jaren the only one
   who really hugs me anymore.
So, I don't push him off.
I say, "Shake it off; you brave, li'l man!"
He sniffles a little, but soon he's done crying enough to
   show me his toy car and his owwee.
This silly dude lifts his Band-Aid-covered leg
   for me to kiss.

"Nah, man." I laugh. "I ain't kissin' that!"

Jaren laughs, keeps trying to make me do it.

But then he gets me.

He leans in and kisses my cheek,
right where *my* owwee is.

FLOW

I finish all them homework sheets and leave 'em
on the table for Ma to see. I play *2K* till I get hungry.

After a huge bowl of Cap'N Crunch, I get a text from Ma.

Don't forget to take out the trash.

I text her okay and get dressed,
   swim trunks under my jeans.
Since Ma works where she works she gets a special pass
to the Brookside Recreational Center. B-Rec.
I put the pass in my pocket, grab my key,
   pull that loud, stinky can
to the end of the driveway, and

I'm out.

EB

To my Ebony princess,

   Babygirl, I miss you more than you could ever
imagine. I think about you and your li'l bro and

sis every single day all day long. Y'all are why I
keep pressin' and never give up, no matter what. I
could focus on the past and be out here feelin' all
depressed and regretful. . . . Is that a word? Or I
could get excited about the future and seeing you in
just a few months.

I think y'all are gonna like Texas. It's big, just like
they say, space to stretch and grow.

Can't wait to take Court to the barbershop that's
close by and you and Aubrey to get your hair done.
We're gonna get ice cream and catch movies and make
burnt grilled cheese sandwiches, just how y'all like.

Babygirl, I hope you know how much I love you.
I know you being strong, cuz you just like me. So
we gonna keep being strong together. Things are
different, but love doesn't change.

I love you, Ebony Princess.

Love,
Daddy

FLOW

Must be my lucky day, cuz there's some
    homeschool group
going into the B-Rec at the same time as me.
I slide in behind those kids, holding my breath
    as I scan the card

and follow them to the boys' locker room.
I skip the shower, just pull off my jeans and stuff them
    into a locker.

The chlorine smell is strong, but I love it.

I never dip my toes in the water to test it.
My dad said that's for punks.
I head right to the diving board and jump in.

The water shocks me every time.

Myesha be cryin' when the water's too cold, but
it always makes me smile, even underwater.

I swim till my lungs 'bout to explode.
Then I spring up, takin' in all the air I can.

"You're fast," one kid says.

I nod. Catch my breath. Tell him thanks.

I'm not the best swimmer in the world, but I'm good.

When I'm in the water, everything just

flows.

EB

I read Daddy's letter three times in my mind
    and once out loud.
Who writes letters, right?
        Text, call, or email, right?

I wish he was here, wish he chose a different job,
wish Texas wasn't where they sent him,
or that Texas wasn't so far from here.

Summer in Texas is what I tell myself. . . .
Summer in Texas . . .

makes my eyes swallow tears while I fold the letter up.

It will be good and bad to say peace to Brookside.

Sometimes it's easy to think about Daddy
    like we was just
together yesterday.
Other times I feel like he's more miles away
in my head than he is in real life.

FLOW

I coulda stayed at the pool all day till they shut it down,
but once the homeschool kids started climbing out,
I knew I better get out, too.
The boys are kinda goofy, joking and laughing
    in the locker room.
I skip the showers again, use my hoodie to dry off.

I walk out before the rest of them and one of the
    workers walks by and goes,
    "You guys are here Wednesday, right?"

Catches me off guard but at least I say,
   "Yeah, I think so,"
instead of nothing.
Maybe the suspension won't be so bad if I can swim
   Wednesday.

EB

Angie never logs in to the doc today. Kianna either.
They on to something new.
Good thing I don't even care.

I turn off the computer, get some paper
   and a purple pen,
and write a letter—who writes, right?—to my daddy.
I tell him about what happened at school.
The
whole
story.
      Everything.
I tell him if he was here, he coulda handled De'Kari,
who should NOT have put his hands on me.
I say,
If you was here, Daddy,
I bet Mama would be, too.

Yeah.

No way she'd be with the guy who's at 1771 Morton . . .
   not with Daddy around.

Hard to be a brown-sugar princess
   without a brown-sugar king.

I don't say that part, but I sho am thinking it.

I tell Daddy I miss him and can't wat to see him.
Then
        I rip
the letter up and throw it away.

FLOW

It's cold outside. Makes me dread the walk home.

So I stop halfway, at the gas station, to fill up on heat
   and pretend like
I'm there to buy something.

Can't believe who comes in a few minutes after me.

Bryce.

Dude must be psychic.

"Yo, what up, D?" he goes, giving me dap.

"You skippin' again, bro?" I say.

"Nah," he goes, with a sly smile. "Got suspended.
      Had a lighter."

I give him a look. Knowing him, he had
    more than a lighter.

"You been playin' *2K*?" Bryce asks.
I shrug. "A li'l."

"Bet," Bryce says. "Anyway, I got three days. I'm gonna
come by tomorrow to play, aight?"

I shrug again, even though Ma would lose her mind
if me and Bryce was gamin' all day.

Bryce grins and starts browsing.
Five finger browsing.

I can feel the cashier's eyes move like a magnet,
        attaching to Bryce and me.

Can't believe the same thing is happening again.
And that even though I coulda got warm a li'l longer,
and I have enough change to buy some Hot Fries,
I walk out the door and move faster toward home.

EB

Don't know why but I love the smell of coffee.
Daddy took us somewhere once,
    I don't remember where,
but I remember seeing coffee beans
    and smelling coffee smells

and for real for real loving it, asking to buy coffee beans
just so I could smell them whenever I wanted.
　　"Uh-oh," Daddy said.
　　"You gonna turn into a coffee head?
　　　　I'ma hafta start calling you
　　　　　　my li'l coffee bean?"

I told him yeah! Cuz coffee is the color of me.

Granny drinks coffee every morning,
　　black and a tiny bit of sugar,
and Poke be bringing those fancy ones from Starbucks.

Latte this and frappé that and sometimes she stingy
　　and don't let me taste.

But today, she brings Starbucks cups of hot chocolate
for me and Aubrey *and* Courtney. Granny fusses, says,
"They don't need all that sugar, 'specially before dinner!"

But we take them cups and swallow quick,
　　heating up our stomachs.

I share with Jaren, who too little to get his own cup.
I don't even care if he backwash.
We all just so happy for this small thing, hot chocolate.
How Poke know that today, right now,
I needed this?

FLOW

When I get home, I head straight to my room,
pull the shoes from my closet.

Custom Jays,

which I wasn't really into before,
    but since my dad rocked 'em
I did, too . . . right after he gave them to me.

They're white with baby blue. . . . Baby blue, like water,
cuz my dad knew the kind of Flow I want to be.

Only now there are ugly storm-cloud scuffs
    on the right shoe
and a reddish-brown blob on the left.

I should've taken care of this on Day One
    instead of waiting.
But better now than never.
I try and remember what Dad would do.

    Bowl of warm water,
Dawn soap from the kitchen, baking soda??
Not sure 'bout that one. . . .

Mix it all together, scrub gently.

Best part of the shoes was the back and the tongue
cuz somehow my dad got them to write
    "Flow."

My name.

His name for me.

EB

Ty'ree comes home lookin' busted, and when Granny
asks how work was, Ty'ree just sighs
    and shakes his head.
His face says he ain't feelin' the new job, but also that
    he know he lucky to have it.
He got a record, and most places don't hire you
    when you got one.

Granny fixes Ty'ree a plate, and he inhales it
    in about two seconds.
Then he heads off to his room, probably thinkin'
the job ain't worth it.
I heard Granny tell him before that quick money
ain't always the best money.
It was hard for him to believe her.
That's why Domino's, Walmart, Staples, Best Buy
    didn't work.
But Ty'ree's good with his hands, fixin' stuff
    since he was a kid,
so maybe the car place will work out for him.

If he stays there,
    he can stay here.

FLOW

The shoes lookin' better, but I still see the stain a little.

Barbecue sauce.
Poured on my brand-new shoes.
    Ebony Wilson.
Accident?
    Nah.
    No way.

    She did that mess on purpose.

Looked me dead in the face and let that small little packet

f
a
l
l

and cause a major problem.

Truth is, I don't even get it. First, she steps on my shoes,
gives 'em an ugly scuff.

I don't remember what I said to her exactly, but I was mad!

    Brand-new kicks!
    With my name on 'em.
      White!
    From my dad.

Anyway. Eb gives me a look like I'm the one wrong.

Like I messed up *her* shoes,
   and not the other way around.

She went to the table with her ugly friends
   and I tried to scrub my shoes
and the bell was 'bout to ring, so I went
   to throw my trash away
and there she was, in my way again.
And that's when she poured the sauce on my shoes.

> The more I think about it, and I don't want to,
> the more I wonder if maybe
> I did call her the b-word.

DAY FOUR

EB

Granny gone again, and Poke and Jaren still asleep.
I'm bored so I go in Granny's room.

I was lookin' for a pencil. . . .

At least that's what I'ma say if somebody walks in.

But really, it's been almost a week—I need my phone!

Granny so predictable it's almost funny.

I open the top drawer, push past bras and panties
   till I find it.
I close Granny's drawer, creep out her room,
   and don't breathe
till I'm in my room.

I hold the phone for a sec, almost scared
   to turn it on at first.

When I finally do, it's kinda like I'm seein' it
    for the first time.
Once it's on, I feel the buzzing
Buzz
Buzz
        Buzz
            Buzz
                Buzz
                Buzz
Messages rolling in, stuff from Snap, IG, TikTok,
    and everything else.

I smile, catching up on short videos that go on forever.
There's a lot of
    Are you okay? texts from Kianna and other people.

I open a text from a number I don't know and that's when
I see it for the first time.
        The video of the fight.

FLOW

I spend all morning on my phone, and noon comes
before I even know it.

In the kitchen, there's a pack of Mr. Clean Magic Erasers
and a note from Ma on the table.
        I want the walls clean by the time I get home,

the note says, and I swear the words on the page
    sound like her.

She trippin', is what I think first.
But since I also know she ain't playin',
    I eat some toaster waffles and get to work.
Never noticed how crappy the kitchen walls are until now.

I play music and scrub and scrub, which really ain't fair,
cuz most of this mess is from Myesha.

Once I finish the kitchen, I move to the hall,
    which isn't as bad.
I'm working on a black scuff
    when there's a knock at the door.
I think it's the Amazon guy, cuz Ma orders stuff
    every other day.
But the knocking keeps going, so I finally go to the door.

Man, my brain and everything else is telling me it's a
    bad idea, bad idea
but I still let Bryce in.

EB

I'm numb and hot and mad and embarrassed
    when I watch.

I flinch and almost drop the phone when I see De'Kari
    hit me.

And I feel sick hearin' everyone go "Oooooh!" and
   laugh and cram closer, like vultures . . .
wanting to see a good fight.

But what really pisses me off when I play the clip again
is Kianna.
She's laughing with everyone else,
   jumping up and down,
      pushing to get close so she can see,
      yelling something,
      but I don't know what.

And it hits me harder than De'Kari that maybe
she really is fake and not friend.

FLOW

"Your moms got you scrubbin' walls?" Bryce laughs.

Why did I let him in?

"Take a break. Let's game."

Bryce wanders to the den and I follow him,
   Magic Eraser still in my hand.

      "You got snacks?" Bryce asks.

"Nah, bro," I say. "You can go home for all that."

"Chill, bro!" Bryce laughs again. "Just make sure
   my walls is clean!"

"Need to clean them Goodwill shoes," I respond.

Bryce fake-laughs, and tosses me the remote.

   "Yo mama work at Goodwill."

I shake my head at the best he's got.

I turn the system on and we deep in a game,
trash-talkin' like crazy before I know it.

"Man, you sure y'all ain't got no food?"
   Bryce asks again,
making a face and rubbing his stomach all extra.

"Shoot, ya mom work at Popeyes," I say, which is all true.
"I know you got some chicken or somethin'."

Bryce misses a three, my team gets the rebound,
   lobs it across the court,
and my guy throws down a dunk.
The game crowd goes wild and I barely hear Bryce say,
      "She ain't been home in two days."

"Where she at?" I ask.

Bryce shrugs. We play for a little bit longer, then make
   huge bowls of Froot Loops from Ma's "secret" stash
   in the laundry room.
We switch games, and the time disappears again.

When I hear the garage door open, I feel three things all
   at once:
   1. Relief—cuz *my* mom came home
   2. Guilt—cuz Bryce ain't have *his* mom in
      two days
   3. Terror—cuz my mom IS HOME!

EB

I call Kianna every ratchet name I can think of . . .
   in my head.
I type and retype a text to her about how fake she is
and about what happens to fake people.

      And then I send it.

I send one to De'Kari, too, on Instagram.
Call him the same name he called me and more.
Feel better, but only a little.
Kianna texts right back:
   What wrong wit u?
   I ain't fake.

Whatever.

When I think about it, it was Kianna who said,
   "Ugh, he act like them shoes

gonna stop him from bein' ugly!"
    while we were at lunch that day.

It was Kianna who said, "Eb, you should go pretend to
    spill something
on his ugly shoes!"
And since he had *just* called me a name when I
    accidentally stepped
on his shoes, I grabbed the small pack of barbecue sauce
and marched over to his table where he was sitting
    sideways, one leg under, one leg out.
I was ready to pretend-spill just to mess with him.

But the pack was open in the corner so when I went
    "OOOOPSSS!"
        all loud and extra,
        a dribble of brown sauce fell in slo-mo and
plopped on the white part of his shoe.

FLOW

    "Yo, you gotta go!"

Bryce knows better
than to be
around when Ma comes in,
so he don't argue.

He cusses;
I rush
to get the room lookin' like we
were never here.
I open the front door
and push Bryce out
as soon as I hear
the garage door
closing.
  Our garage is
  detached,
  and so is
  my heart,
  thumping and
  jumping
  cuz Ma
  still gotta
  walk
  to the back door
  and I'm
  hoping
  Bryce goes
  the opposite
  way.
I dash
to the den,
pick up
the Magic Eraser

from the floor
where I dropped it,
and scrub a wall
like
my life depends on it . . .
　　　cuz it does.

When Ma walks in
she stares
at me
so long
I just know
I'm busted.
I'm not
expecting her
to say,
　　　"You over here lookin' like the Black Mr. Clean!"

I suck my teeth,
　　go, "Maaaannnn,"
but it's
probably
the first grin
on her face
since what happened
happened.

EB

I'm the type of person who don't cry for nothin'.
Not for whuppin's, not when a teacher yells at me,
not when I'm on punishment,
and not even when I get in a fight.

There was no tears when De'Kari caught me in the face.
No tears when Daddy moved away,
   made Texas his new home.

      I'm tough.
         Gotta be.
But after I call my
   mama and get her voice mail
   two times in a row,
   big stupid TEARS splash onto
   the picture of
   me and her on my phone.

FLOW

Ma got me choppin' onions, which I hate, and Myesha
   got the easy job of rinsing carrots and broccoli.

We're making Ma's All-Together soup,
   which is really where
she dumps a bunch of leftovers together and
   makes a soup out of it.

You would think it's nasty, but it's always amazing.
Ma puts some serious magic on it . . .
    that's what my dad would say.

"This enough?" I ask after I have a mound of onions.

"Yeah, that's good," she says, which is my cue to go.

My phone has been charging in my room and
    when I grab it,
I see a message from Ebony.

        How she have my number? How I have hers?
I don't even remember.

But we definitely ain't friends right now.
I read the words she called me, the words she
    called Ma,
        who is just making All-Together soup in the
            kitchen,
            not bothering nobody.
I get mad.
    Quick.

So I text back.
    Quick.

I tell that girl exactly what she is and what she can go do
    and even though
that tiny TINY voice in my brain says to maybe
    NOT send,
        FLOW, DO NOT SEND!

Guess what . . .
I send the text anyway.

EB

I'm wiping those stupid tears when my phone buzzes
and I swipe away from Mama's face to my messages.

Everybody thinks De'Kari is this quiet kid who don't be
   botherin' nobody.
But if they could only see the mess he textin' me.
My mood swings from sad and weak to pissed and strong.

     Who this li'l boy think he is?

I make myself numb to his words, and I refuse
to let them hurt me again.
At all.

So I don't respond.

But I decide that when Ty'ree gets home I'ma tell him
   I need De'Kari taken care of.

FLOW

Can't shake the feeling I feel, so I ignore it.
Eat three bowls of All-Together soup, wash dishes,
take a shower, and read a book for an hour
   like Ma tells me to.

Whole time, I glance at my phone, wondering what mess
Eb gon' text me next so I can blaze her, make her pay
   forever
for the stain on my shoes and for everything else that's
   wrong.

But yo, she don't respond and that's almost worse than if
   she did.

EB

Aubrey coughs and cries all night long
    whenever she sick,
so I ain't get NO sleep!
I kept my whole face under the covers so her germs
    don't get me.

I hate being sick.

When it's light and I look over at her bed, I see a pile
of snotty tissues all over the floor like snow.
Now she'll be whining all day, and Granny gon' make me
drink the same gross garlic and grapefruit tea that
    Aubrey gon' have.
I can already hear Granny's mouth if I complain:
    "If you was at school
like you supposed to be, you wouldn't have to worry
    'bout no tea."

Which is a lie, cuz Granny would make me drink that
   nasty tea
even if I was going to school.

Sure enough, Aubrey start her snifflin' and whinin'
   a few minutes later.
I tell her to shut up and go find Granny, which she does,
lookin' pitiful as she slumps out the room.

Since Granny will be busy with her, I slide my phone
from under my pillow and turn it on.
No messages from Kianna. Dang, she could at least
say she sorry or something.

I text Angie and then get on TikTok for a while.
I don't get to see Angie's message cuz Granny calls me
and I gotta turn this thing off quick and go drink that tea.

FLOW

Now that Uncle Reggie is done with all that
   early-morning stuff,
I sleep in peace and get ready to go to the B-Rec.
I know it's risky—there's a chance I get played—
that the homeschool group don't come or that they come
at a different time but I go anyway.

I walk fast cuz it's cold, and I'm thinkin' 'bout the water
   the whole time.

I started swimming lessons when I was three cuz
    my grandma—my dad's mom—lost a brother to
    drowning.
Because of that, she made my dad and all my
    uncles and aunts and all the cousins, ALL of us,
    learn how to swim early.

I don't remember much about the lessons,
    but I remember this one time
my dad picked me up and threw me in the pool.
I was scared, but only at first.
Then all the good stuff kicked in and I was
    moving through that water like a shark.

"That's it! That's it!" Dad yelled from the side.
"He goin' to the Olympics," he told Ma, laughing,
    but for real.

When I come up for air after swimming a few laps,
a guy with a huge brown beard is standing at the
    shallow end,
arms folded, watching me.

        I'm busted.

I picture the look on Ma's face and the
    beatin' she's gon' give me
when she finds out about this.
I wanna hide underwater.

"You got nice form," the guy says. "You swim for anybody?"

I'm not all the way sure what he means,
    so I just go, "Nah."

The guy nods, strokes his beard.
    "The rec has a youth swim league.
You should check it out."

I don't say nothin', just stare at this dude.

"We have flyers at the front, but first, you probably
    wanna catch up with your group."

That's when I notice the last few homeschool kids
climbing out the pool.

"Oh. Yeah."

I scurry out the pool and hurry to the locker room.
But if I could, I would stay in that water all day.

EB

Granny doin' her best to keep Jaren from Aubrey
    and her cooties.
All that means is now he stuck to me like glue.
We chill in Poke's room, since Aubrey's
    taking a nap in ours.
"Wanna read dis one!" Jaren says,
jamming *If You Give a Mouse a Cookie* in my face.

"Aight, aight!" I tell him. We read that book four times

before I hide it under Poke's bed when he ain't looking.

We draw for a while, until he yawns.
"You sleepy?"
He shakes his head, yawns again.

"Go lay down," I tell him. And he does.
　Climbs up on Poke's bed
and is out in two minutes.

I clean up the mess he made so Poke won't have
nothing to say when she gets home from work.

I'm putting pens and pencils on her dresser
when I see a bunch of her pictures.
Mostly selfies, but also of her and different guys.
She always looks cute; them guys always look
happy to be standing there with her.

Granny calls Poke *fast,* been calling her that since forever.
She don't call me that.
People got a whole other word for me.

　　　Bad.

Nobody would believe a boy actually likes me.

But one does.

Trey Karson.

So as I look at Poke's pics of her and different guys all
　boo'd up,
I start imagining it's me and Trey instead.

FLOW

St. Vincent's Academy has a swimming pool
   in the school,
which means a swim team, too.
If I cross the bridge and walk forever, I'll get there.
Gigantic school. Even the grass is perfect.
If it wasn't so cold out, I would walk over there right now
and imagine it's my school and my swim team.
If my grades were better and I didn't have so many
   suspensions and referrals,
maybe it would be
         my school,
         my swim team.

I fold up the pamphlet for the Brookside Rec Center
   Youth Swim League,
put it in my jeans pocket, and walk home,
   tryna figure out how to tell Ma about this
   so I can join without telling Ma *all* about this.

EB

"You got him to take a nap?" say Granny,
   whispering as she peeks in Poke's room.

I nod, glad I wasn't still staring at Poke's pictures
   when Granny came in.

I pick up all Jaren's scribble papers, and when I look over,
Granny's still standing there, watching me.
My first thought is she knows I took my phone.
But she don't say nothin' about that yet.

"Got some chicken noodle soup," she tells me,
   which I know means I gotta follow her downstairs.

Granny got the table set for three, but then she pours
   Jaren's bowl of soup back into the big pot.
I sit down, take a slurp, before Granny fusses at me
for not saying grace. "You know better."

We eat without talking;

Granny's the first to say something.

"That boy takes forever to lay his behind down for a nap.
You must have the magic touch, Eb."

I shrug.

"I just told him to lay down, and he did," I say.

"He loves you," Granny says. Smiles. "You always been
real good with him."

I keep my face the same, cuz I don't know where Granny
   is going with all this.
Probably just gonna make me watch him more.

   "Whatcha think 'bout being a teacher one day?"

I almost drop my spoon.

"Granny, you trippin'!" I say, shaking my head.

"Naw, I'm sitting here just fine in this chair.
    Not stumblin', stutterin', trippin', nothin'!"

Granny tryin' to be funny.

"I ain't dealin' with no bad kids all day," I tell her.

"Who said they gotta be bad?" Granny demands.

"In all my thirty-eight years of teaching,
    I ain't met not one bad kid."

I don't believe her. Shoot, even Mama said I was bad,
last year when I got in trouble for taking
    Ms. Rainer's phone.

That was right before Mama moved with her boyfriend
and us to Granny's.
"Can't deal with these bad kids,"
I heard her say under her breath.

I told myself she ain't mean it . . . she was just upset.
Aubrey and Courtney always be messin' stuff up.
Me too, I guess.
But maybe she did mean it.
It is true,
I am bad,

Granny's wrong.

"Think about it," Granny says. "You got a teacher's heart."
I almost ask Granny what that means, how she sees that,
    how she know.

But I keep my face the same and finish the soup.

FLOW

I can tell her it came in the mail. I can say
I got it at school, before the suspension.
I could even say I found it.

But what I can't do is tell Ma I been sneaking out
to swim at the B-Rec.

My cell vibrates as soon as I get home,
and my first thought is that it's Ma.
But nah, it's Cas.

"What up, bro?" he asks.
"Nothin'," I say.

"You sound real guilty!" Cas laughs.
    "What you been up to?"

"Chillin'," I say.

"Mmmm-hmmm," Cas says, like he don't believe me.

"Yo, anybody home? I'm about to roll through."

"It's just me; you good," I say.

Cas be avoiding the house when
    Ma or Uncle Reggie are here.
They both stay on him about doing something better
with his life and all that.

To me, he's doing a lot—he got a job and his own place
and even a car.

He has a roommate or two, but he says it helps with rent.

The car's kinda raggedy, but Uncle Reggie
keeps it running.
Other than more school, I don't know what else
they want him to do.

Cas comes by like ten minutes later and immediately
checks out the fridge.
"Ain't nothin' in here!" he says.
"Let's go get burgers!"

1. I know for sure there's leftover meatloaf in the fridge.
Bagels and All-Together soup, too.
2. It feels weird to think that I might have to ask Ma
if I can hang with my brother.

But since I already snuck out without Cas
3. I might as well go with him, cuz
4. A burger from Larry's sounds real good
right about now.

One thing about swimming—it makes me wanna eat
everything in sight.

At the drive-thru, Cas orders two of everything.
Deluxe burgers, fries, root beer, pecan pie.
We drive home and smash.

I eat the burger, onions and all,
    cuz it would be kinda rude
to pick them off in front of Cas, who paid for all this.

We put all the Larry's trash in a separate bag
and push it way down into the garbage.
Not that it matters. Whole house smells like Larry's.

"You been gaming?" Cas asks.

"Yeah."

"Not enough to beat me," he says.

So of course, I gotta prove him wrong . . . or at least try to.
Unlike Bryce, Cas doesn't flinch or jump
when we hear the garage door.
He just kinda sighs, says, "Here we go," under his breath.

Few seconds later, Ma and Myesha step into the house.

"Cas!" Myesha yells, jumping into his lap.
He laughs and tickles her.

"Yo, you gettin' big, My-My!"

"So are you!" she giggles.

Once all that settles down, Cas glances over at Ma
and nods. "Hey, Ma."

"Hey, back atcha," she says.

I'm holding my breath, hoping they don't start fighting.
Myesha must feel it, too, cuz me and her start lookin'
from Cas to Ma, praying she'll say the one thing
that makes everything okay.

"You stayin' for dinner?"

EB

Granny on this teacher thing so much that she
    makes me help Courtney with his homework.

Man, second grade is easy compared to seventh.
I don't see why he cryin' and complainin' about
adding and subtracting two numbers on top and
two numbers on bottom.
He don't even have to carry or borrow all the time!

I show him how (even though he already know),
and once we got that worksheet done,
we have to read a book for his li'l reading log.

"I don't wanna read that!" Courtney says.

"So? Nobody asked you if you wanted to. You have to.

So read!"

"It's too hard!" Now Courtney whinin', and
I hate when li'l kids be whinin'!

"It don't matter; once you finish it, it won't be hard
no more cuz you'll be tougher and smarter."

Granny walks by the table when I say that,
and I see a smile on her face.

Well, I know one thing—I ain't 'bout to be no teacher!
I would lose it if I had a classroom of Courtneys
to deal with.
Nah.

No
Way.

DAY SIX

EB

I sent Trey a text last night. It was just to see what's up.
He didn't respond until late so I don't see it
until now....
> Snow day! wyd?

I blink and sit up. Aubrey's still huddled in her bed.
Granny put the humidifier in our room, and I can see the
cool mist floating around.

I get up and look out the window.
> Yup, buncha snow everywhere.
> Man! That means both Courtney AND Aubrey will
> be here
ALL day.

I stare at Trey's text and send one back.
> Nuthin, just wakin up.
Trey texts:

Gonna be at my cuz house ltr. U shud
come thru.

Trey's cousin Jonny lives near Ma.

Kids be hangin' there all the time.

Would be nice to see people instead of being
cooped up on a snow day.

I'll see . . .
    is what I text Trey.
He sends a thumbs-up emoji.

Now all I gotta do is figure out how to get away from
  Granny.

FLOW

Uncle Reggie goes in on me for five minutes straight.
He's all, "Boy, I just shoveled y'all's whole driveway
while you in here, asleep.
Man up!"

How am I supposed to know it snowed?

Uncle Reggie stay trippin', talkin' 'bout how I'm
  supposed to be
the man of the house since my dad's gone.

But I don't wanna be no man of the house.

I just wanna be me.

Ma comes in my room next. "Uncle Reggie's taking me
to work," she says.
I chuckle and she gives me a look.
Ma's low-key scared to drive in too much snow.

"Myesha's gonna be here with you."

Ma tells me to
        make sure I don't sleep too long,
        make us some oatmeal for breakfast,
        stay off the game and pay attention to Myesha.

Myesha's seven, not no baby that I gotta "watch."
But Ma gives me *another* look, so I just say
"Yes ma'am" and shut up.

Myesha wakes up excited and dances into the kitchen
wearing some kind of ballerina mess.

"Snow day, snow day! I love snow days!" she sings
in a super-high voice.
We eat and Myesha begs to wash dishes
    cuz she's really into bubbles.

I gotta let her, right?

After that, she wanna play outside in the snow.
What?!

"Nah, too cold," I tell her.

"Pleeeeeassse!" she begs. "You can play video games
   after, and I won't tell Ma. . . ."

Yo, when did my baby sis get so hardcore?

   We bundle up and go outside.

Myesha acts like she never seen snow before!
She rolling around and laughing, jumpin' up and down.
I stand there watching her, hands stuffed
   in my jacket pockets,
Until she throws the first snowball.

Hits me right in the chest.

"Ay!" I yell.
She squeals and laughs and throws another.
I jump out the way this time.

"Yo! Watch out, Myesha!" I warn.
   "You don't want this smoke."

"I don't want smoke, I want SNOW!" she yells in this
loud battle voice.
She's packin' snowballs as fast as she can,
   and I can either take her attack or fight.

Myesha's not ready for what comes next.

I pound her with the snow she wants and yell,
   "NO MERCY!!"

   She loves it!

It's like she gets wilder each time a snowball hits her.

Pretty soon, we're racing all over the front yard
   throwing snow and laughing
till my hands are freezing so much
   I can barely feel them.

EB

Trey has curly black hair and light brown eyes, so
      all the girls been liking him since kindergarten.
We been friends since then, but now it's different.

That day last summer at the B-Rec made things different.

Trey's best friend, Shawn, was sick that day so
Trey hung with me like old times.

Back when we was kids our favorite game to play was
      hide-'n'-seek, and I thought Trey was joking
      when he said we should play it

That day.

"Why you laughin'? I'm for real!" Trey had said.

"Cuz it's for *babies*," I told him.

"We not gon' play it the baby way." Trey grinned.
   "If I find you, you gotta give me a dollar.
If you find me, I gotta give *you* one."

I ain't have a dollar, but I was pretty sure I could get one
from Trey.

I was wrong.

I hid behind a stack of folded chairs in the gym and
Trey found me in, like, two minutes.

I laughed, said I ain't have no dollar to give him,
so oh well.

He shrugged, grinned, and kissed me.

"Now we even," he said.

We hid and found each other for the rest of the day
That day.

FLOW

We shake and stomp and brush off snow
    as much as we can
and rush inside, where it's warm.

"Hot chocolate!" Myesha says, and I check to see
if we got any.

Three packs left, and we use them all.

    Myesha burps real loud in the middle of
        drinking hers,
and I laugh.

"You sound like Cas," I say, cuz he burps when he's
   drinking anything.

"I wanna get suspended," Myesha says out the blue.

"No, you don't," I tell her. She's little, just thinkin' 'bout
being at home and that's it.

"Yes, I do!" she says. "But I don't want Mommy to be mad."

"Then be good," I say.

   "You be good!" Myesha says, and it feels like
   another snowball
   to the chest.

I say, "I am."
   I just know she's gonna say something like
"No, you not!" or "Then why you get suspended?" or
something else to piss me off.

But she doesn't. She says, "I know."

   And burps real loud again.

EB

It would be nice if I could text Kianna to brag about
   Trey's text.

I almost click her name, but nah.

I'm gonna do this one on my own, without her stealing all the shine.

I get up and head downstairs, where Granny's watching the news.

> "This mess gonna be bad," she say, maybe to me, maybe not.

I look at the weatherman and at the shot of Brookside down by the library and post office and all that.

> Snow everywhere, coming down fast.

"Hey, Granny," I say on commercial break.

"Hey, Eb, how you feel?"

"Good."

Granny nods. "I been watchin' this here weather; ain't made no breakfast."

"That's aight; I'll eat cereal," I tell her. "Where's Jaren?"

"On the potty," Granny say. "I think Aubrey got 'im sick."

That makes me feel bad, but also glad it ain't me.

Granny gonna have her hands full of Jaren and Aubrey and Courtney today and maybe that works for me.

Sometimes, after lunch when Jaren takes his nap, Granny takes one, too.
This *gotta* be a day that she does.

Jaren's nose is runny when he comes out the bathroom,
but he ain't all whiny like Aubrey. He happy to see me,
and after our bear hug, he wanna build a tower
outta the blocks I got him for Christmas
      with my own money.

Each time he sneezes I hold my breath and fan the air,
which he thinks is hilarious.
We build and build while Granny heats up soup
and that nasty tea.

Aubrey whines her way downstairs in a blanket.
She's holding a box of Kleenex for dear life.

"Be quiet!" I tell her. "You already got Jaren sick,
and he ain't whinin' about it!"

"I sick!" Jaren says.
Aubrey sniffs and slumps onto the couch.
When Granny comes in, she feels Aubrey's head.
"I told Ty'ree to get some Tylenol on his way home.
I surely ain't going out in all this."

But Granny got it wrong.
I rather be out there in all that than in here with all this.

No more cootie house for me.

FLOW

Snow day means no school, so I leave that homework
packet to rest in my room and I get on my game.

Myesha don't even bother me.
She's off doing whatever she does in her room,
which is what our deal was anyway.

When I game, my mind just kinda floats,
   like when I'm in a pool.
I'm not worried 'bout nothin'.

Bryce jumps on 2K, and we battle.
He wants to hang, go get snacks from that gas station,
      and probably do some other stuff, but I tell him,
"Nah, I gotta watch Myesha."
He say to bring her, too, and I go, "Nah, we good."

I make ramen noodles for lunch and Myesha says
   it's the best . . .
better than Ma's, Dad's, Cas's.

Yeah, Myesha, it is.

I play 2K for a little bit after that, but then I end up
on my phone looking at St. Vincent's Academy's
swim team videos on YouTube.

I see a dive I wanna try next time I sneak to the B-Rec.
Watching these dudes, I know I gotta get fast fast fast.

Blink and I'll be gone. The only thing I'm wondering is,
are they gonna make me wear those teeny tiny trunks?

EB

I make a pack of ramen noodles for me and Courtney,
the only ones not sick.
Aubrey's still asleep on the couch, sick-snoring,
and when I go to ask Granny if she want some,
I find her with Jaren ASLEEP!

This my chance!

"You not eating? Where you going?" asks Courtney
when I leave my bowl of noodles on the table.

I pull on my coat, search for my boots.

"If Granny wakes up, tell her I gotta do something
for school. At the library."

I have to tell him three times what to say cuz Courtney
be all over the place.

"What I'm suppose to do by myself?" he asks.

"Take a nap," I tell him, borrowing one of Ty'ree's hats.
"Or watch TV. Just keep it on low."

Courtney's cool with that.

I check Granny one more time . . . still asleep.

I grab my phone and I'm out.

FLOW

"Mommy's home!" Myesha warns me before Uncle
    Reggie's truck turns into the driveway.
Nice of her. Too nice. She probably gonna play me.
I gotta get some dirt on her.

I turn off the game, slip my phone in my pocket,
and make myself look busy in the kitchen.

"I see you been out to play, but not out to shovel,"
            goes Uncle Reggie.

No "Hey nephew, what's goin' on?"
No "That's cool, you was playin' out there
    with yo baby sis!"
No "Y'all hungry? I brought pizza."

Ma at least tells me hi before she calls Myesha
to make sure she's okay after a day with me.

"Get your coat and stuff on," Uncle Reggie says.
"We gonna knock this driveway out."

Uncle Reggie. Ma's big brother. I wonder if that's
    the kind of big brother I'll be in twenty years,
    lookin' out for Myesha and being super hard
    on her kids.

Uncle Reggie moves his truck while I open the garage
and grab shovels.

One long, long path down the middle slicing the
driveway in half just like Dad used to do.

Then side to side, fast as I can cuz it's freezing and
I don't have a mechanic jumpsuit and mechanic boots
like Uncle Reggie does.

"I'ma hafta get you a suit," Uncle Reggie calls.
"Your li'l chicken legs are shiverin'!"

Ha. Ha.
Not my fault I grow fast and last year's snow pants
went to Goodwill.

"You know we probably gonna have to hit this again
in the morning, right?" Uncle Reggie says.

"Maybe it'll stop snowing," I go.
I hate
Hate
HATE
waking up early to shovel, and I wish Dad was here
to do it instead of me and Uncle Reggie.

I'm facing the garage when Uncle Reggie says, "Hey, now,"
and I think he's talking to me.
But when I turn, I see he's just saying hi to this girl
who's stomping down the street like she's mad.

It's too cold to be walkin' around, but I guess I don't
mind it either when I'm walking to the B-Rec.

EB

Granny believes in long johns like they're the Bible,
and for once I'm glad she does, cuz I put some on
under my jeans.

It's cold out here and I wish I was in one of those
kid snowsuits that cover everything.

At least I don't have to shovel, like this kid and his dad
on Oakland Street.
A man from the church does Granny's for free.

The snow comin' down, but not as fast as before.
The swirls make Brookside look gray.
They also make things seem quieter.
I make a rhythm outta my steps:
crunch-crunch
       crunch-crunch
       crunch crunch crunch crunch
Repeat.
If I had gloves, I'd add a muffled clap.
But my hands gotta stay in my pockets to be warm.

So I just stomp.

Poke got me the boots from Rainbow for Christmas,
but they cute boots, not snow boots.
My two pairs of socks are starting to feel wet.
I pull my coat tighter and make my feet go faster.
Maybe this ain't such a great idea.

FLOW

The ONLY good thing about shoveling snow is that it
  makes me super hungry
  and Ma ALWAYS has something tasty
and warm when we get inside.

Uncle Reggie stays for chili and corn bread and the
  chocolate chip cookies
that you get out a package and put on a pan and bake
  for twelve minutes—
    aka the best kind.

"It's still bad out, Reg," Ma says, peeking out the
  window.

"Guess I better head on home, then," Uncle Reggie says.

But Ma makes him some coffee, starts up some
  long story about Grandma and my auntie Keisha
  and this lady Toya from back in the day,
  who was *almost* my auntie by marriage,
    until Uncle Reggie found out
    she liked to run up credit cards,
and they sit and laugh at the table long enough
for Ma to convince Uncle Reggie
to just spend the night.

EB

Right when I get to Trey's cousin's street—Woodward—
a horn beeps loud, twice, and makes me shiver
    from shock, not cold.

    "Ebony? Ebony!"

It's Mama.

MAMA.

Her car slows down and she peers from the window.
My mouth falls open.
It
is
really
    her.

    "Whatcha doing out here?"

"Hey, Mama!"

    "Get in the car!"

I hurry to the passenger side and climb in.

Her car is warm and clean and smells like smoke.

She's playing music that Granny would
    frown and fuss about.

"You just gettin' out of school?" she asks, driving
down Woodward, past Jonny's house,

where I stare real hard to see if I see Trey
   and try to not trip off Mama's words
and the fact that she don't even know
      I'm suspended.

"Ummm, I was just walkin' to my friend's house."

      "From your granny's? In all this snow?"

"I have to do something for school.
   Like, a group project."

"Hmmm," goes Mama. She turns onto Parker,
   then King,
then Morton.

And then she pulls into 1771 Morton, where the
   driveway is a mess of snow.

Mama huffs, goes, "That fool ain't even shoveled?"
She must be talkin' 'bout Marc, her latest boyfriend,
who ain't *nowhere* near as good as Daddy.

Daddy woulda had the driveway shoveled
before Mama got home.

I think we gonna get stuck going into the drive.
   But Mama guns it,
and we cut tracks in the snow.

"C'mon," she tells me, opening her door.
I follow her up the steps, and then I'm in her house.

It's nice, cozy, more smoke smelling but also vanilla,
Mama's favorite scent.

Mama yells to Marc about the driveway,
     and he yells something
about being busy and 'bout to do it in a minute.

I stand at the door, not sure what to do.
Mama fusses some more, then walks toward . . .
     the kitchen?

"I made chili, Eb!" she calls.

Don't have to tell me twice.

I slip off my boots and follow her voice.

Mama's dishing me up a bowl, sayin',
     "Bet you miss this, huh?"

I tell her, "Yeah, I do."
          I miss
          a lot
          of stuff.

The chili's real good, good enough for two bowls.
Now I'm feelin' so warm and cozy that my mouth
     stops chewing and goes,
     "Mama, can I spend the night here?"

Right away, I hate that I said it.
Hate that she prolly 'bout to shut me down,
make me look dumb for asking.

My heart freezes, and I stare at the last spoonfuls
   in my bowl
so Mama won't see the water in my eyes.

   "You should call your granny, let her know."

Wait . . .
      Wait . . .
                WHAT??

"For real? I can?" I don't even care how little-kid-excited
I sound.

"Yeah, you can stay the night.
You for sure ain't walkin' back,
and I for sure ain't driving you."

Mama tells me to call Granny, and I almost do,
   until I remember
I'm not supposed to have my phone.

"Um, can you call her?" I ask, thinking fast. "My phone
   been trippin'."

And for the second time today, Mama says
yes.

FLOW

Not
gonna

lie;
we
sleep
better
with
Uncle
Reggie
here.

DAY SEVEN

EB

Marc has two little girls who are five and six.
I sleep in their room and try to be happy I'm here
and not mad that Mama puts up with his kids
but not
hers.

"Get up, Eb," Mama says, waking me up
(but I'm already woke).
"Gotta take you to Granny's."

It's another snow day for us kids,
but Mama still gotta work.
IHOP don't close for snow. People still need
their pancakes, I guess.

Mama's assistant manager, and when I told Granny
I'm gonna work there, too, she was all,
"Naw, you ain't!"

Mama gave me a T-shirt and leggings to sleep in,
   and I pull my other clothes over them.
Marc's sipping coffee in the kitchen when I get there.
    Smells of leftover IHOP hit my nose.
      "Hey, Eb," Marc say.
"Hey."

He makes me a plate of dry, crusty hash browns
   and two floppy pancakes.

      "So you suspended, huh?"

I narrow my eyes. Mama told him?
   Me and her talked about it last night,
   but I ain't think she would tell *him*.

I pour syrup on the pancakes instead of answering.

Marc goes, "Yeah, that used to be me. . . .
Don't even worry 'bout it, baby."

Well, I wasn't worryin' 'bout it
   till yo' big mouth said something,
I think.

I look around for Mama, hopin' she come in here
   and tell this fool
to mind his business.
      "Guess I better get to this driveway, 'fore your mama
      be runnin' her mouth," Marc say.

He put his coffee cup in the sink and grins.
   "Got an extra shovel,
      you know."

I give him the biggest stank face. "Nah. You got it."

Marc bust up laughing.
   "Girl, you said that jus' like yo mama!
         Look jus' like her, too!"

Good, I think.

      Good.

FLOW

Surprise #1: The driveway's done, and Uncle Reggie's gone
         by the time I wake up.

Surprise #2: Ma's home. She makes waffles and eggs
   for breakfast,
says the snow is so bad and she needs a day off.
Nice.
Except for the fact that I prolly won't be gaming today.

      After breakfast Ma makes me get to that
      school packet
      (even though it's technically another snow day).

"You only got three days left, 'Kari," Ma says.

"You gotta be thinkin'
'bout what you gonna do different. You can't keep actin'
    a fool at school."

I smirk a li'l bit, cuz of Ma's rhyme,
    but she raises her eyebrows,
    says, "Is something funny?"

"No," I say quickly. "It was just, 'fool in school,' a rhyme.
    Get it?"
    Ma's face says she is NOT impressed. "De'Kari—"

"Nah, you right, Ma," I interrupt. "I'm not tryna mess up
    no more."

"Uh-huh, you said that last time."

"I know."

I think about Mr. Warren saying I'm close.

My grades go
up
and suspensions
        go
        down
and I get on the honor roll, then maybe St. Vincent's
will take me.

I think about the papers from the rec center and
    I'm just about
to go grab them, show Ma that

Flow
    got
       Goals

when her phone rings.

And the way her face lifts when she answers tells me
   that
     it's
       Dad.

EB

Mama's car is nice and toasty cuz Marc started it up,
   which I guess was pretty nice.

    "Eb." Mama sighs. "You and all this trouble!"

I stare out the window as we drive,
   try not to feel too bad when Mama sighs again,
   like I'm really stressing her out.
Before yesterday, she ain't even know I got in trouble.
Granny the one who deal with all that.

Now I *am* feeling bad.

Is Granny dealing with me and
   Aubrey and Courtney and Poke
cuz Mama don't want to?

"How come we don't live with you no more?"

I fling the question like a curveball
　　nobody's expecting. . . .
Not even me.

Mama keeps her eyes straight ahead,
　　doesn't speak at all.

So I get like her—LOUDER.

"Why, Mama? How come we gotta live with Granny?"

　　　"Ebony, don't start with all that."
　　　Mama waves her hand
　　　　　but it don't wave my question away.
I stare at her with laser beam eyes, and I
KNOW
she feel it!

　　　　Mama's tough, though.

She don't even glance over.

If I didn't see the way her hands clench the
　　steering wheel,
I would think she don't even care.

My phone (that I'm not supposed to have)
　　buzzes with a text,
and since my mama's trippin', I look.
　　　It's Trey.

wyd

I text.
Still wit my mom.
I smile cuz he texted yesterday that he thought
I was comin' through, which means . . .

You miss me, huh
I send my message with a smiley face emoji and
   Trey sends a smiley face back.

     "Who you over there grinnin' at?" Mama asks.

What I wanna say:

     "Mama, don't start with all that!"
     like how she told me.

But I wipe the grin off my face, put on a smirk instead
   as I send Trey
   the kissy face emoji and say,

"Nobody."

FLOW

   Deployed.

Moved into action or position.

   Sent far away.
There's lots of definitions for this word I hate,
   but for Ma and Myesha and me,

all it means is
   gone.

Dad's voice is staticky and Ma strains her ears
   to hear him.
She smilin' and smilin' and nodding to whatever he sayin'.
I don't hear his words for real, but I can hear his voice;
the deepness of it cuts in and out of all that stupid static.
Ma tells him something about her job,
   and while she doing that,
I go get Myesha.

Here's how we do it: Ma talks first, then Myesha,
and I get Dad last.
A few times, the phone cut out during my turn.
Going last is risky, but I like to be the one to tell him bye.

      Today, though, I'm kinda nervous.
He way way way across the world,
   dealing with real serious stuff,
and he don't need to be hearing 'bout me getting suspended.

I'm praying that Ma don't tell him.

Myesha got her notebook of "Things to tell Daddy,"
   and I swear,
she goin' on and on and on about silly stuff!
   Classmates, the snow day,
   the tacos we had a few days ago,

the hairstyle Ma gave her,
the frozen squirrel some kid found on the playground.

I'm 'bout to snatch the phone from her hand
   but Ma jumps in,
gives me my turn.

     "What up, Li'l Flow! Voice gettin' deep!" Dad goes,
     after I say hello.
       He lyin'!

     "So what's new with you?" Dad asks.

"Nothin'," I say, when the answer is really "A whole lot."
I wonder how Dad gonna feel 'bout me wanting to swim,
wanting to go to St. Vincent's instead of Brookside High
like him and Ma and Cas and everybody.

I almost slip and tell him about swimming at the rec
but I look up, see Ma watching me.

I wanna say something about school,
   but I ain't been to school. . . .
So I swallow that down, too.

"It keep snowin' here, they keep closin' school," I say,
feelin' dumb cuz Myesha already told him about that.
"Maaaan, it's blazin' hot here!" Dad says,
   with static and a smile.
"All I wanna do is jump in a pool of ice water!"

Me and Dad laugh. I'm thinking 'bout what that ice water

would feel like, how hard it would be to swim in.

"School going good?"

"Uh, yeah. Yeah." I catch Ma's eyes again.
   She looks away.

I tell Dad about being close to honor roll.
   Ma raises her eyebrows,
but it ain't a lie.

Dad tells me to keep it up.

   And then I feel it.

I always be feelin' the moment when he gotta go.

Last thing he says is "How them shoes holding up?"

Dad was here for Christmas but it wasn't long enough.
I know I wasn't supposed to, but I heard what he said to Ma
the night before he left.

Same night he gave me them shoes.

I heard.

"They good," I tell him.

EB

The look on Granny's face when I get home
  makes me freeze
in the hallway.

It's not really mad. . . . It's a mix of sad, worry,
  and me letting her down.

"Granny—"

    "No one knew where you were." Granny speaks
    soft and strong.

Turns out Courtney forgot the words I told him to say
  and went with
"I don't know where she is" instead.

    "You think running away is—"

"Granny, I ain't run away! I was walkin' to the library—"

    "And I musta been born the day before yesterday!"
    Granny shakes her head.

I keep my mouth shut while she talks about the path
I'm on (even though my feet right here in the house!).

The worst thing?

When Jaren come running in to see me,
  Granny sends him right back
  where he came from and
  lectures me some more.

"And you went trespassin' in my bedroom, Ebony?"
Granny's eyes really flashin' now.

"I—"

"Don't you speak another lie!" Granny shouts,
pointing a finger at me.
"I've had it with the lies and the fights and the
sneaking and stealing!
THAT'S IT!"

Granny walks away, just leaves me standing at the door.

What Granny mean? She don't want me here?
If I can't stay with her and I can't stay with Mama,
where else I'm gonna go?

Does Granny want me to go?

Maybe I will!

Seem like nobody cares anyway.

I turn around, push the front door open.

I'm on the porch, I'm on the steps, I'm on the sidewalk.

My phone buzzes in my pocket. I snatch it out.
I see who's texting. (It ain't a text.)
I bust out crying. I take the call.
It's

Daddy.

FLOW

Dad always says, "Aight, boy, keep it flowin',"
when we 'bout to get off the phone.

Today he says it and asks to speak to Ma.

I go to my room, pull out the shoes, clean 'em again.
Unfold the B-Rec flyer, read it again.
Ma comes in while I'm still looking.

"What's that?"

I pause big-time, don't wanna tell her 'bout me sneakin'
to the pool.

"Um, they gave us this at school," I say.
   "Before . . . you know."

Ma takes the pamphlet, reads it real slow.

"Ain't been to the rec in a minute," she tells me.
   "Membership and all.

You interested in swimming?"

I nod.

"I love swimming."

Ma stares at me. "You was always real good in the water,"
she says.

"That's why I'm Flow!" I say.

"That's why you're Flow," Ma repeats.

She stands and pats her stomach. "God knows I need to be in the gym!" she mutters.

Ma takes the pamphlet with her when she leaves my room.

I think that's a good thing.

Keep it
    Flowin'.

EB

At first, it's just me cryin' that ugly cry and Daddy going,
    "Eb! Baby girl, talk to me. Ebony, what's the matter?"

Cryin' in the cold ain't no joke.
My face so cold it feels like it's on fire!
My words are frozen, too.
I gulp, try to just "breathe and allow things to pass"
like they tell us in school.

It kinda works ... but Daddy's "Eb, I'm about to call your
    granny on three-way" works even better.

I take a deep breath. . . .

"Daddy, I wanna come live with you," I say.

Daddy's quiet for a second, and I think he prolly 'bout

to give me an answer like Ma's, or no answer at all.

"Baby girl, I can't wait for you to come in the summer,"
   he says.
"If you like it when you come and you feelin'
   the same way . . .
      we can go from there, okay, baby?"

I tell him okay; he ask me what's really wrong.

What's really inside me is the feeling that
   nobody wants me.
But I can't make myself say them words out loud.

"I just miss you," I say. "Granny mad at me."

"Nah, she ain't," Daddy say. "Your granny? She be lovin'
on everybody. And she just want the best for everybody."

Daddy prolly right, but I ain't never seen Granny this mad.

I wipe my face; the crying helped.

"Something just told me to check on my baby girl,"
   Daddy say.
I can hear him smiling.

I smile, too. Me and Daddy, we always been
   connected like that.

"I'm glad it was you, Daddy," I say.

"Who else it gonna be?" Daddy say. I laugh.
      It *could* be Trey, but I don't dare tell Daddy that one!

Daddy asks about Aubrey and Courtney, and I tell him
   about Aubrey being sick.
He know how that go.

"Wasn't thinking you'd answer. They let you
   be on the phone at school?"

Shoot!

Guess I gotta tell him. . . .

"I'm suspended for fighting."

Daddy gets quiet, but at least he don't go,
   "Again, Ebony?"

"What you gonna do different next time?" he asks me.

"Not fight," I say.

It's getting colder out here. I walk up the porch steps.

"And how you gonna not fight?"

That makes me have to think about The Fight,
which I'm not tryna do.

"I don't know." I shrug, even though
   Daddy can't see it.

"*I don't know* means it's gonna happen again.
Think about the moment things went wrong.
What could you do different?"

Maaan, c'mon, Daddy!

"This boy called—"

"Nah, Eb." Daddy cuts me off!
   "We'll deal with 'this boy' in a minute.
Right now, it's just about you."
   Granny comes to the front door,
and I ain't never been happier to see her.

"Girl, get inside this house!" she say.

"That your granny? Lemme speak to her."

Maaaan!

"It's my dad," I tell Granny,
   stepping inside the warm house and
handing her my phone and
   knowing I prolly ain't gonna
      see it again.

FLOW

Ma let me game after I did a bunch of pages
   out the packet.
Bryce on here, talkin' a bunch of trash,
   but he don't want this smoke.
I blaze him in *2K* game after game, and he still
   runnin' his mouth!
Brandon and Jay-Jay on here, too, clownin' Bryce hard.

My fingers freeze on the controller when Jay-Jay laughs

and says, "Dang, you beat his butt like you did
    that ugly girl at school!"

They crack up but I been tryin' to forget
    that whole fight thing,
especially since I gotta be at school in a few days.

"Chill," I say. But Bryce don't listen.
    He take the heat off him,
and goes in on Ebony, retelling the whole thing,
    adding stuff
that ain't even happen.

"Her face went BLAHHOOOWWW!"
Bryce says, all loud.

I flinch. *Ain't like I meant to hit her,* I think . . .
only I didn't think it. I say it out loud.

"Man, whatever! She deserved it! Messin' up
    your new kicks like that!"
Bryce says.

"That was foul," Jay-Jay adds.

Then they back to the fight, exactly where
    I don't wanna be.

"Yo, my mama say I gotta get off."

The guys clown me, but I don't care this time.
I log off my PS4.

What do I do now?

DAY EIGHT

FLOW

Snow decided to chill out, which means no more
    snow days for Myesha, and since Ma's at work,
    it's a quiet house for me.
Ma leaves me a note about how maybe next weekend
    we'll go to the B-Rec.

Next weekend? It's Monday!
    We need to be going today!
I text her to ask.

After 'bout an hour she texts . . .
We'll see. Make sure the kitchen is clean.

I swear, Ma be doing some blackmail type stuff.
I could clean this kitchen so you see yourself sparkling
    on everything,
and she would still come home talkin' 'bout

"Sorry, baby, maybe tomorrow."

I clean it anyway.

EB

Granny keeps my phone, just like I thought.
I don't know what Daddy and her was talking about,
but Granny didn't do no more yelling.

Jaren real happy I'm back. His li'l sick butt
    snuck into my bed this morning and fell asleep.
He feeling a lot better but his breathing still kinda raspy.
I pat him when he cough in his sleep.
At least Aubrey's at school, and I don't have to hear
her whining.

I smell bacon downstairs.
Granny know that's my favorite. . . .
Wonder if there's any left.

Jaren's arm is slung over me, and I try to move without
waking him up but his eyes pop open.

    "BeeBee," he say with a sleepy smile.

"How you feel?" I ask him.

    "Hungwy!"

    "Me too."

Jaren scrambles out my bed, grabs my hand,
    and a few seconds later

we running down the stairs, Jaren yellin' for Granny.
She in the kitchen with Poke. Poke?

"You not at work?" I ask.

Poke shake her head, sips from a mug.

Granny's face looks tight!
   I hope they both ain't mad at me still.

"I hungwy, Mama!" Jaren says, bouncing up and down.

"I can fix him something," I volunteer.
There's a plate of bacon on the stove. Yes!
I grab the bread and make Jaren and me some toast.
Slice up some bananas and strawberries, too.

Poke and Granny don't say nothing the whole time
and it feel real weird.

"I'll be back later, Poke," Granny finally says.
   She puts on her coat and hat and boots,
   and leaves, even though she don't really like driving
   in the winter.

"She still mad at me?"

"Not just you," Poke says. She puts her mug in the sink
and walks out.

Huh? What is goin' on?

Jaren eat like he don't notice anything different.

But different is all I feel up in here.

FLOW

I watch TV after the kitchen's done,
   but nothing good on.
Bryce and them prolly wouldn't believe me,
   but it's getting
boring at home.

Uncle Reggie calls from the shop.
   "What you over there doing?"

"Nothing."

"Yeah, right! You wanna swing by the garage?"

Honestly? "No."

Uncle Reggie cracks up. "Stay out of trouble, nephew."

"I will."

Not much trouble to get in at home.

I'm eating Frosted Flakes—ooooooh, dangerous!—when
   Bryce texts me that Jay-Jay got in a fight
with Malachi Burton, this eighth grader,
during passing period.
He sends me a clip that has a lot of yelling and cussing
and moving around, but I can't really see the
   actual fight.

They lucky.

They won't have to spend their ten days with their fight
on everybody's phone.

Bryce also tells me that Sherese Little asked him when
    I'm coming to school.

> **She miss you, bro!**
> **Guess it's gonna be your beatdown**
> **comin' next!**

Bryce adds some laughy face emojis to his message.
Whatever.

Sherese this girl, she cute, she smart, she good at
    ball, and
everybody scared of her daddy.
He a bus driver, and out of all the buses
    for Brookside schools,
he drives the one I ride.
We gotta say, "Good morning, Mr. Little"
    each time we get on,
and if we don't, he make us get off and try it again.
Sherese got two sisters, and the rumor is he beat
    one of their boyfriends so bad
the dude moved away and changed schools.
Rumor is he snatched up Mr. Warren,
    had him up against the wall,
when he tried to suspend one of them for cheating.

Rumor is he got security cameras all inside their house,
   outside, too.
And now rumor is,

Sherese checkin' for me?

EB

"Poke, you get fired?" I ask when I take Jaren
   up to her room.
He got a lot of energy right now,
   so it's time for his mama.
Poke layin' on the bed, scrollin' on her phone.
Lucky.

"No," Poke snaps. "And why you so nosy?"

"Then why Granny mad at you?"

"She ain't mad."

Yeah, right. Granny revved the car up when she left,
   like she was
happy to get away.

"I might go stay with my dad," I tell Poke.

"No, BeeBee! No!" Jaren attaches to me like a leech,
and for the first time I think, do I really wanna go?

Only cuz of Jaren.

"Boy, I don't mean right now," I say, peeling him off.

Poke watches me.

"Why you wanna do that?" she asks.

I shrug. "I wanna get away from Brookside.
    Tired of the people here."

Poke shakes her head, goes to her phone.
    "People is people
everywhere, Eb. Same people gonna be in Texas."

Nah. If I'm in Texas with Daddy, won't be no more
    stupid De'Karis and fake Kiannas
    and busy Mamas and angry Grannies,
    and that's exactly how I want it.

FLOW

I'm chillin', watchin' TV, and there's this movie called
    Pride that I almost pass by,
    but I see this kid dive and since it's
    about swimming, I watch.
A swim team at a rec center back in the day.
    There's this part where

the team is practicing and they ain't even in the water!
One guy is just laying on a bench,
    pretending to be swimming.

I laugh at first, but then . . .
    I move the thing we put our feet on
while we on the couch
and I lay on it, move my arms
like I'm swimming . . . and feel real dumb.

But since nobody's home, I think, yo, why not?

I keep moving my arms and legs, imagining that I'm
    slicing through pool water instead of air.

After a while, it's not so dumb anymore. Just because
I'm not in water don't mean I can't swim.

EB

It feel weird without my phone.

You would think I'd be used to it by now.

I wanna see if Trey texted but Granny got smart—
musta found another hiding spot.

I get on the computer and check my school email.
Nothing important. Nothing from Kianna.
    Don't know why
I keep checking for her.

Angie and Precious at least emailed me a few times to
    see if I was okay and to let me know
    what's been goin' on at school,
but their last emails were three days ago.

Guess people forget quick.

FLOW

Fake swimmin' makes me almost as hungry as
    real swimmin'!

I finish the movie and call Ma,
    ask her if I can order pizza.
At first, she tells me pizza is for sons who ain't
    suspended.
        Pizza is for sons who do their chores.

I take a pic of the kitchen while she's rambling
    and text it to her.

She stops midsentence. "What about your room?"

"It's clean."

"Your homework?"

"Ma, I finished that packet yesterday."

        "Mmmm-hmmm."

Sigh. Ma likes making me wait.

"I'm telling the driver to leave it on the porch.
Don't you open that door
till they're in their car. You hear me?
And save some for when My gets home."

I say "Yes, ma'am" a million times before Ma
    makes sure
a large Double P is comin' my way.
    Pineapple and Pepperoni.

        That's how Flow do it!

I count to ten when the doorbell rings and peek out the
    window to make sure the lady's in her car.
Then I open the door, grab the box,
    and devour about half of the Flow Special
    before Myesha gets home.

This girl picks off the pineapple *and* the pepperoni!

"Yo, you ruining the Flow Special!"

Myesha rolls her eyes. "It was already ruined."

Dang.

"You a hater," I tell her. "A plain-cheese hater."

Myesha just shrugs and eats her pizza slice with dents
where the best stuff used to be.

EB

Granny don't come home for a long time.
Poke orders pizza for lunch cuz she don't feel like
   cooking and she don't want my bomb noodles.
   Whatever!

When Granny do come back, we all can tell she ain't
   'bout to be playin'.
"I want everybody in the living room," she says.
   "Ev-er-y-body!"

She stretches that word out, and I'm like,
   Oh boy, here we go....

Granny even wakes Ty'ree up,
   tells him to get his narrow behind
to the couch. Dang! She pissed!
   Granny usually lets him sleep
a little on his days off.

We all here—me, Jaren, Aubrey, Courtney, Poke, and
   Ty'ree—
and all of us quiet like we in church.
Granny don't even say nothing for a while and I start
to get real nervous.

What if
   she still mad?
   she got cancer?
   she tired of us living here?

We all holdin'
our breath,
waiting on her
to talk.

"I been thinking long and hard
'bout the state of this house.
What we doing right and
what we doing wrong.
I had to go and get
prayed over cuz
Lord knows
I'm at my
wit's end.

    "One thing I'm not gonna do
    is have confusion and dysfunction
    in my own house! There is enough of that
    out there waiting for you. From now on, we
    function as a team that got some sense! No more
    foolishness! No more! Won't be no more cutting up
    in school or smart-mouths or not doing your chores
    and messing up my house!
    And we going to church *every* week, maybe twice!"

Ty'ree groans and Poke rolls her eyes
  when Granny says that part.
Wrong
move.

"Oh, you got a problem with church? You got a problem
    with getting good grades and not fighting everybody
under the sun? Then I suggest you start calling around,
see who else you can stay with."

Granny's like the Energizer bunny; she keep going and
    going on and on about how things are gonna be.
    "Now we got another family member coming,
and I will not have confusion in my house!"

Huh?
Another family member?

"Is Mommy gonna live here?" asks Courtney,
    all excited,
        too excited.
        He don't know no better.

"Stop askin' dumb questions!" I tell him,
    mad that it's a dumb question.

"Then who's coming?"

Granny don't answer, but I see her eyes drift over to
    Poke.
Granny goes, "Hummph!" and shakes her head.

Poke?

My sister's lookin' down.
    Picking at something on her hoodie.

"Poke, you pregnant again?" I blurt out.

"Dang, Granny, you just put her business in the street!"
   says Ty'ree.

"The street is exactly where all of y'all will be
   if you keep up this mess
   in my house!"

Ty'ree closes his mouth.

Dang, Poke's pregnant? Jaren gonna be a big brother?
I got another nephew or niece?

"Lord knows I want my babies and their babies
   safe, happy, and whole.
Lord knows I rather have y'all here.
   But we got to do better, family.
We got to *be* better."

We all lookin' around at each other, probably all
   thinking
the same thing.

   We do.

DAY NINE

FLOW

Cas wakes me up today by farting right by my face!

"Ugh, gross!" I yell, holding my nose with one hand
and punching him with the other.
Cas is laughing like a hyena,
   acting like he four years old!

"Get up, bro!" he says. "Ma told me your hair is
   lookin' a hot mess! We goin' to the shop."

I groan big time.

I hate the shop.

Don't matter if you got an appointment or not,
you always gonna end up waiting.

Once, Ma dropped me off and, no lie, I sat in there
for three hours for a twenty-minute cut.

"Nah!" I say, pulling the pillow over my face.

"Ain't no 'nah,' " Cas says. "You gotta be fresh
when you go back to school."

Oh.
Snap.

School.

Tomorrow.

Our school does this stupid thing where you gotta
   spend the last day of your suspension
    in the ISS room, talking about
how you gonna make better choices.

I'm hoping it won't be just me and Ebony in that room.

Now my whole day is messed up.

EB

Poke home again today; I guess she been feeling sick.
Granny said she gonna mess around and lose her job,
   but I don't think Poke cares
'bout all that right now.

She just tryin' not to throw up.

After she wake up from a nap,
    she comes downstairs yawning,
says she'll braid my hair for school.

Poke always been good with hair, better than Mama, even.
She does mine and Aubrey's and Jaren's,
    cuz he got braids, too.

"You gettin' in all these fights, you need to keep your
    hair cornrowed,"
Poke tells me on the first braid.

She right. I fought this girl Lanise once,
    and she went right for my hair.
Can't lie, I went for hers, too.

"You ever get in fights?" I ask Poke.

"Not really. Only a few."

Figures. I bet Poke ain't have nobody messing with her,
calling her names.

"You excited? About the baby?"

Poke keeps braiding.

"I sho ain't excited about this morning sickness!
    I didn't have that with Jaren."

That don't really answer my question, but I guess it also
    kinda does.

FLOW

Yo, I'm shocked that the shop ain't so crowded.

Usually, the place is packed, and you gotta stand around
   waiting for a seat, waiting for Big Mo to finally say,
"Aight, you next."

Today, only three other guys are inside.
   Li'l Mo's cutting one guy,
and Big Mo's got the other. Third guy waiting.
   Hopefully,
I won't have to wait, too.

"What up, Big Mo!" Cas says when we walk in.

"'Ey, Cas, good to see you, young brotha!"

Cas nods to Li'l Mo. If you smart, and you been in
   Brookside all your life, you know that Li'l Mo aight;
   he just ain't nowhere near as good as his dad.

"I got you up next, li'l man. Although"—Big Mo eyes me—
"you ain't so little no more!"

"Nah, he ain't!" Cas says. They laugh and Big Mo talks
   about how he remembers Cas at my age.

Big Mo's old, like, grandfather-old.
Old enough to remember
what my dad was like at my age, too.

He tells a story 'bout my dad trying to cut his own hair
and the disaster it turned into.

"Your daddy would be in here rappin' up a storm,
gettin' more tips than me!" Big Mo tells me,
dusting off his client's neck. (Yes! He almost done!)
"How he doin'? Y'all heard anything recently?"

"He good," I say. I (try to) make my brain forget
  what I heard.

Dad did sound alright on the phone.

"That's a blessing," Big Mo says. He takes off the cape.
His client pays. I should be up next. . . .

"Say, y'all mind if I get him in real quick?" Big Mo asks.
He's nodding to the guy in the waiting chairs.

"Nah, that's cool," says Cas, probably just to make me mad.
"Li'l Flow ain't got nowhere to be, right, bro?"

Cas elbows me and I swear, if he opens his mouth about
my suspension, we fightin' in here.

"I can get you in a sec, Cas," offers Li'l Mo.

I almost choke, tryin' not to laugh. That's what Cas gets!
His face looks like, *Awww dang, how'm I supposed to
  get out this one?*

People be feelin' sorry for Li'l Mo,
  don't wanna tell him no.

Shoot, I would tell him in a heartbeat.
If I gotta wait five hours for a cut, it better be a
    Big Mo cut.

EB

When Poke get finished with my hair,
    I chill out in front of the mirror
with a grin on my face. Poke always hooks me up,
    even though the braids
are pullin' my scalp SUPER tight!

"You gotta pick out a fiyah outfit, too, Eb. Go to school like,
'I'M BACK, Y'ALL!'"

When Poke say that, the smile slides right off my face.

School.

"I don't even wanna go to that raggedy school,"
    I mutter.

"You'll be aight, girl," Poke says.
She tryin' to make me feel better, but I don't.

I'm all in my head 'bout what people gonna say.

Poke must be in my head, too, cuz she goes,
    "Shoot, don't let nobody get you off your game."

    "How I'm supposed to do that?"

"Stay focused on *you* not *them*."

I nod, thinking about them: Kianna, De'Kari,
    De'Kari's stupid friends,
Mr. Warren, Ms. Humphries.

But I already know somebody's gonna have
    something to say.

Which means I'm gonna need to have
    something to say, too.

That's just how it go.

FLOW

An hour later.

That's when I finally get in Big Mo's chair.
He wraps the cape around me just as the
    barbershop door opens,
and I swear, if he asks me to wait again . . .

Yo. Mr. Guidry in language arts always be talkin' 'bout
    tension
and rising action and how that stuff changes a story,
and right now Big Mo's shop is filled with so much
    tension.

I don't know the dude at the door or the dude with him,
but their faces look like Aces and those faces drift
toward Cas.

"How y'all brothas doing?" Big Mo says, and I can hear
    the difference in his voice. Tight. Hard. Suspicious.
He's holding the clippers but not buzzing them on.

"What up, Big Mo," the first guy says, still watchin' Cas.

Cas stares them down. He don't move at all (except for
his jaw clenching) but he still finds a way to make
himself seem stronger, harder, ready, just by being still.

"Y'all can have a seat," Big Mo says. "I got you
after these two."

"Nah," the second guy says with a snort. He still
glaring at my brother. Nobody even looking at Big Mo.
"We be back, when your *other* customers is gone."

Dude's words hang in the air like Jordan,
    slam down hard like Shaq,
and when those two pass on Li'l Mo's offer
    to cut their hair,
    and walk out the shop,
        I feel like we just
        beat the buzzer like Kobe.

EB

One thing I love about my sister is that she's
down for whatever, whenever.

"Let's go to the mall," she tells me.

"Right now?"

"Yeah, right now! While I feel aight."

I guess that whole morning sickness thing
is really messin' her up.

Only problem with this plan is that Poke don't have a car,
    which means she's gonna have to ask Granny.

"The mall?" says Granny, making a face. "What y'all
    need at the mall?"

"I need some jeans. Eb needs a nice outfit for school,"
Poke explains.
"Can I borrow the car?"

I can already read Granny's mind. *All the mess y'all
    sisters done got into, and you think*
I'ma let you take my car to the mall?

"Eb got plenty of clothes," Granny says.

"She need something special, Granny. Trust me."

Granny waits a second.
Two.

Maybe it's because Granny was a teacher, and she knows
how it is after kids get suspended.

Maybe she's been suspended before. . . .

Or maybe she do trust Poke.

I guess it don't really matter which one it is

Cuz Granny gives us the keys.

FLOW

Cas is looking all around when we leave the shop with
     fresh cuts and go out to his car.
We climb in and he takes off,
     but we don't go far.

Cas turns into the rec center parking lot.

"You in trouble with them Aces?" I ask, point-blank.

Cas's voice gets dark. "Aces always lookin' for trouble."

That don't answer my question.

"You know them?"

"I know who they are," he says.

"Why was they mean-muggin' you like that?"

"You been comin' here by yourself?" he asks me,
     ignoring my question.

Okay.

I act like him. No answer. We sit like that for a minute.

"I rather you be right here than out in the streets,
li'l bro."

"Like you?" I say it, but I'm also hoping it ain't true.
Cas ain't out in the streets.
He got a job, got a place, got a car.
Never really gets in trouble like I do.

Cas stares at me hard.

I stare at him.

"What you wanna know, man?" he finally says.

"I wanna know what's up with you and those guys.
They're Aces, right?"

"Yeah, they are. They got beef with me
over a female," Cas says.

"Whatchoo mean?"

"Grown-folks bidness."

"Not if I'm 'bout to get caught in some cross fire!" I say.

Cas got me messed up. People go out like that all the time.
Wrong place, wrong person.

"You ain't gonna get caught up in nothing!" Cas tells me.

I believe him I believe him
Do I believe him?

Cas must see my brain spinnin' cuz he lets out
   a huge, heavy breath
and spills the tea.

"I hung out with this girl a time or two. Didn't know she was with ol' dude from the shop."

"The Ace . . ."

"Yeah, the Ace. So now the girl pregnant or whatever and ol' dude think it's me."

Oh.
Snap.

Cas was right. Grown-folk bidness.
I did NOT wanna know.

"Get out the car, man," Cas says. "Let's see what your jumper talkin' 'bout."

I climb out and Cas go, "What you grinnin' for?"

"You 'bout to see," I tell him, cuz if we go in here, it ain't gonna be about no jumper.

EB

Poke power-walks right by the Rainbow in the mall, makin' a face even though she don't work at that one.

"Ugh," she go, "I don't wanna be up in that store."

So we go to other stores instead.

Journeys and Bath & Body Works and Claire's and this
    new store called StreetHeat, where we get jeans
    and this sales boy named Darius
flirts with Poke.

We get his employee discount and he gets
    a fake number from her.

We eat pretzels from the food court and
    drink a mix of, like, six pop flavors,
and everything feels like it used to,
    when Poke first got her license
    and let me go places with her and her homegirls.

    "She's soooo cute!" is what her friends would say.
And Poke would go, "I know, right?" And they would
all crack up laughing when I said smart things to adults.

It was funny then.

I do that now and I get suspended or sent to the
    Focus Center
or told to watch my "smart mouth."

Smart means something different now.

"We should see a movie," I tell Poke,
    cuz I don't wanna leave just yet.

I got school tomorrow, and I don't wanna
    even think about it.

Poke nods, but a few seconds later, she
runnnnnnssssss
to the nasty public bathroom.

I follow her, but wish I didn't. I hate the sound
and smell of throw-up.

Poke comes out the stall lookin' tired and sad.

"We can't do no movie, Eb," she tells me.

But I already knew.

That's just me bein' smart.

FLOW

Cas stares at me for a good minute when I tell him
I wanna swim, not hoop.

Bro, we don't got no trunks! is what he says, but someone
overhears him and tells us
    they sell swimsuits at the front desk.
I'll pay you back! is what I promise Cas,
    and he pulls out his wallet

and buys two pairs of too-expensive swimming trunks.

Cas mutters the whole time we changing, but I barely
    hear it.
Can't believe how hyped I am to hit this water. . . .

So hyped,
I don't even wait for him to jump in.
So hyped,
I swim some quick laps, and it feels like I barely
   come up for air.
So hyped,
I don't hear Cas calling me at first;
   he's just an echo in my mind.

So hyped, I'm grinning when I finally stop,
   and all I need is a few breaths before I'm ready for more.

"YO! You ain't hear me callin'?"

I'm just breathing and grinning, grinning and breathing,
feelin' at home in this pool.

"When you get so good?"

I shrug, then say the only thing there is to say:

    "Wanna race?"

EB

"God, I wish you could drive!" Poke say for, like,
the ninth time.

I know she mean it, too, cuz she asked me at the mall
if I wanted to drive us home.
I almost said "yeah" even though I would be nervous,

but before I could say anything, Poke said, "Neva mind," and slumped herself behind the wheel.

We driving mad fast, cuz the mall is thirty minutes away
    and I can tell all Poke wants is her bed.

When we get to Granny's house,
    Poke leaves the bags for me to carry inside,
and when I get there, Granny's shaking her head.

"Lord, help these children," she mutters,
    hand out for the keys.

I grab Jaren, who's pounding on the bathroom door
for his mama.

"Jaren, relax, boo boo," I tell him. "Your mommy ain't
feelin' well."

"He can sense the other baby," Granny says
while I kiss and tickle him.

"For real?"

"Poor thing gonna have to grow up quick."

I study Jaren. He's so small and cute . . . can't imagine
him gettin' all big and stuff.
I hope he stay a nice, good boy and don't get in
    no trouble.

"You gonna be good, Jay?" I tickle his tummy and he
    squeals, says yes.

"You gonna stay nice?"

"YES, BEEEBEEE!"

I hate that my mind thinks about De'Kari and his friends
for a split second. I wonder if they said the same thing
when they was Jaren's age.

I gotta make sure my nephew don't change and be
    like them.

DAY TEN

FLOW

Uncle Reggie wakes me up early, talkin' 'bout he's
    driving me to school.
    He ignores everything I say about taking the bus,
which means he's gonna lecture me the whole way there.

I get dressed slow, cuz I gotta decide if I'ma wear

    the shoes.

    I cleaned them again yesterday,
    after I beat Cas in lap races
three times in a row. I felt like that guy in that movie. . . .
    He couldn't touch me!

We were starving after, so burgers and fries and
    milkshakes from Larry's.
    Cas said I cost him a lot in one day.
Cost.

I pull the shoes out.

They don't look too bad. I think about what my dad told Ma,
in a

    l

       o

          w

whisper the night before he left.

They were hugging. I shouldn't have heard it:

> *"Baby, I have this feeling. . . . A feeling that*
> *I'm not gonna*
> *make it back next time."*

I slide the shoes on.

EB

It don't matter how good my hair looks
   or how fly my new outfit is,

I do *not* want to be in this room with this boy.

We ain't the only ones in ISS, at least.

    In-School Suspension.

Some sixth grader is here, too.

"Come in and take a seat," says Mrs. Rashad,
   with her big eyes, African head wrap,
   and jangly bracelets on her wrists.

She ain't stank like Ms. Humphries,
  but she's nosy and she be makin' kids cry.

  Not me.

Dang, I know the drill, Mrs. Rashad!

    Come in quiet, turn in work,
    sit down quick, eyes up front.

Check, check, check, check.
Except I give De'Kari a dirty look on my way to a seat.
I make sure I sit behind him and on the opposite side
of the room so he don't try nothing.

Mrs. Rashad takes attendance, which is a joke,
  and she's giving
the same tired "expectations" speech when the door opens
and Mr. Warren barges in.

"Good morning," he says to Mrs. Rashad. Then he says,
  "Marquel Banks?"
and the sixth-grade kid jumps. I snicker.
  Must be his first time.

"What is your first-hour class?" Mr. Warren asks.
"Science," the kid says. "With Mr. Burton."

"I suggest you get there," Mr. Warren says. "And let this
  be your last time in ISS. Understood?"

Man, this corny kid actually says, "Yessir!"
  and scurries out the room like it's something scary.

Ain't nothing scary about ISS.

"Miss Wilson and Mr. Flood," says Mr. Warren.
"This will also be the last time you visit our ISS room."

"Good," I say under my breath. Mr. Warren stares at me
   but pretends he doesn't hear.
   "If either of you have any more behavior infractions
at Brookside Junior, I will be referring you to
   Horizons Academy."

I almost laugh out loud—Mr. Warren got me messed up
   if he think I'm going to that school!
   It's even more raggedy than Brookside!
      Horizons Academy, where we all know
         the bad kids go.

My laugh don't get out all the way, though,
   because I can tell he's dead serious.

My heart beats faster, my hands get sweaty,
   my eyes blink twice,
but I suck my teeth and roll my eyes like I don't care.

      I DON'T CARE!!!!

I can't let anybody know I don't want to be sent away.
Can y'all just stop sending me away?

FLOW

My dad has this thing with feelings.
He had a feeling he was gonna marry Ma
  when they met in high school.
He had a feeling he was going to Iraq before they told him.
He had a feeling I was a boy before the ultrasound.
He had a feeling something wasn't right with Grandma
  before she died.
He had a feeling about Myesha way before Ma was even
  pregnant.

Dad's feelings don't be wrong.
  I could always count on that. . . .
Now I don't want to.
  But I think maybe I got some of that
feelings stuff, too. . . .

When that girl Ebony comes into the ISS room
  all stank-face,
    I get the feeling that this day is only gonna get
    worse.

EB

There's a stack of work for me and De'Kari
  on Mrs. Rashad's desk, but she says,
    "Before we get to all that, let's talk about this," and writes
    PEACE on the board.

Dag, for real? She 'bout to be on some
   "hold hands and sing" mess; I can feel it.
   She gives us these journals and tells us to
   write the first things that come to mind when we think
   of that word.

I write *NOT ISS* and when Mrs. Rashad asks us
to share our words, I tell her,

"Being up in here disturbs my peace."

Mrs. Rashad raises her eyebrows. (She never yells like
   other teachers.)
"That's funny; you're in here so often, Ebony, I thought
   maybe ISS is a place that brings you peace."

De'Kari snickers, and I whirl around
   and tell him to shut up.

Mrs. Rashad raises her hand, reminds us of the
Expectations in the ISS room.

"It's just the three of us. No one else to entertain," she says.

Entertain?

I'm not some class clown. I only clap back when
   someone comes at me.

Mrs. Rashad talks about Martin Luther King Jr.,
   of course (his whole birthday thing just passed),
   and how he was peaceful and nonviolent and all that.

But while she rambles on, my eyes drift with my mind
 and I see
a picture I never seen before.

It's a picture on a book.

A girl.
A Brown girl.
Alone.
In a sea of not-brown faces. Angry faces, loudmouths
all around her.
Nobody watching out for her.
Nobody walking with her.
Nobody seeing she's only pretending to be brave.

Mrs. Rashad passes out our work packets, says we got
 math for the next hour,
but I can't stop looking at that picture.

FLOW

Yo, I don't know if I'ma make it through this day
 in this room.
Ebony trippin' already, tellin' me to *shut up,*
 with yo' ugly shoes!
I swear, I'm not trying for déjà vu, but it's probably
gonna happen if we trapped in ISS together all day.

I raise my hand, ask to go to the bathroom.

Uncle Reggie said to use my head today, not my fists,
to be at peace, not at war.

At peace, not at war.

That's what I wrote in my notebook.

Dad's at war so I can be at peace.

Mrs. Rashad gives me the pass, tells me not to get
  lost. (Ebony says something under her breath, can't
  tell what.)

I make a face, open my mouth to say something to her,
but Mrs. Rashad cuts me off, asks me to take a note
to Mrs. Kyles, the music teacher.

"It's on your way," Mrs. Rashad says, scribbling the note.
She has to wave her hand to break the glare
    I'm giving Ebony.

The hallway feels like freedom. I could pull a Bryce
and just be out. Gone. Deuces.

But then it's deuces for swimming at St. Vincent's.

Maybe that's a dumb idea anyway.

I'd probably be like those swim kids in that movie....

Not a lot of Black kids at St. Vincent's.

And that got me thinkin'....

Do I wanna be like them swim-team dudes?

Do I wanna leave to get what I need?

EB

When it's just me and Mrs. Rashad, I ask,
  "Who's that girl?"
My eyes are on the picture, and Mrs. Rashad
  hands me the book.

"I could tell you, Ebony, but I think you'd enjoy
it more if *you* found out."

I almost laugh and say, *You trippin', Miz Rashad!*

But something tells my hand to move,
  so I flip the book open
and read.

Wow.

So Elizabeth Eckford, the girl by herself, was supposed
  to meet up with her other classmates but she didn't get
  a message in time.

I think about me being alone, the only one in trouble. . . .

Kianna and Angie and Precious and all them
are somewhere else.

I look at the Elizabeth girl's face and it feels like
    she's looking
right
        at
            me.

FLOW

Not gon' lie, that walk down the hall helped me out.

Quiet, empty, cool.

When I come back, Ebony's reading and she don't even
    look up.

I work on all these assignments, and she keeps on
    reading and Mrs. Rashad's doing
        whatever it is she does at her desk until 10:30,
    when she tells us to
        stand up.

Huh?

Stand up, reach your arms to the ceiling.
        Stretch, stretch, stretch!

We lookin' real dumb right now! Mrs. Rashad has us
    stretch to the top, the sides, and the bottom.
I can't touch my toes . . . I peek over and see that
    Ebony can.

Mrs. Rashad has us crossing our arms in front of us
and drawing figure eights in the air while we breathing,
and I'm like, when did this become yoga class?
She didn't use to do all this.

"Ooh, my back just cracked! I'm suing the school!"
says Ebony.
Mrs. Rashad smiles.

"I bet it felt good, though, didn't it?"

Ebony doesn't answer.

And when Mrs. Rashad asks her to move up a
   few rows,
she does it.

Now I can see her out the corner of my eye.

She's on my left, plenty of desks between us still.

Good.

EB

Not gon' lie, them stretches felt good. Mrs. Rashad even
had us jogging in place! Yo, this ain't gym!

She says we can do these stretches and all those
   breathing things at home,
even show our parents and siblings.

She says it helps to stretch and breathe and create
    positive energy
when we're angry or frustrated or sad or just too
    amped up.
I'll try it on Jaren when he's bouncing
    all over the place,
and Aubrey and Courtney when they're whining.

The bell rings—lunch—and the hall gets loud.
I'm kinda glad I get to just stay here
in
        peace.

Some kid brings our lunch at 11:43, thirteen minutes later.

Turkey sandwich, chips, apple, string cheese,
some baby-looking cookies, milk.

I hear De'Kari opening his bag and complain.

"Not what you wanted Mr. Flood?" asks Mrs. Rashad.

I wonder why she ain't eating.
    She got one of them shake things,
so I guess she's drinking her lunch.

"Nah," goes De'Kari. "I don't like blue Doritos."

"What?" I stare at him. "Blue Doritos are the best."

"Red all day." De'Kari shakes his head.

"You dumb!" I say. But then I catch Mrs. Rashad's eye.

She don't look happy.
"I mean . . ." I look at the red Doritos on my desk.

"You wanna trade?"

FLOW

One hour left in here, and now Mrs. Rashad wanna talk
    about the fight.

She talks about respect and how that changes
    everything.

Then she shows us a picture. It's that same girl from
    Ebony's book, but she's all grown up
and the girl who was yelling at her in the first picture
is all grown up, too.
Now they have smiles on their faces.

"Of course, I'm not saying you have to be best friends,
Ebony and De'Kari," Mrs. Rashad says.

"Flow."

I don't mean to interrupt,
but it
slips
out.

"Excuse me?"

"I like to go by Flow."

I'm not expecting Mrs. Rashad to laugh.

But she does.

I feel the anger bubbling up inside,
   cuz if *she's* laughing,
Ebony's probably gonna start, too.

"Well, that is just so fitting!" Mrs. Rashad says.
"It's perfect! I'll bet neither of you even realizes it.

Eb and Flow."

EB

Mrs. Rashad won't let this *Eb and Flow* thing go.

She's saying we should be a rap group
   or a singing group
or something.

"Nah, Mrs. Rashad!" we both say. No *way* we
   workin' together
on *anything* like that.

But Mrs. Rashad has us look up the term
   and use what we find
to write a letter to each other.

Like, for real?

"Talk about the shoes, Flow," Mrs. Rashad says.
"Talk about something *you* love, Eb.
How are you feeling about each other?
    Tomorrow, you won't be in ISS, and that's
    when it all counts. That's when you'll put into
    practice everything we've learned today.
Anger?
You can control it.
Words?
You can ignore them.
Accidents?
You can apologize for them.
    You can think before jumping to conclusions."

"You sayin' too much!" I tell Mrs. Rashad.
    I'm not trying to be rude;
she just needs to ease up on all this
    "do this, do that" stuff.

"Then let's simplify," Mrs. Rashad says.
        "Kindness and respect."

FLOW

Uncle Reggie picks me up after school, like a
    kindergarten baby.

Everybody prolly sees me climb into his truck
     instead of the bus.
          And for what? He ain't gonna do this every day!

"How'd it go?"
Fine.

"Any issues?"
No.

"The girl was there?"
Yeah.

Uncle Reggie don't like one-word answers, but my head
still swirlin' from all the thoughts I been thinking
     today.

Last thing we did was write
Kindness
          and
Respect
in our notebooks. What it means to us,
     how we can show it to
each other.

Mrs. Rashad's an okay lady, but I don't know if all that
     stuff gonna work
outside the ISS room.

Kindness
     and

respect
are just words grown-ups love to throw around and
kids don't try to catch.

We go to Uncle Reggie's garage and I get
   harassed right away.

     "Here come trouble!" calls Pete.

"Chill with all that!" Uncle Reggie growls, pointing at
   Pete in a mad threatening way.
Pete backs off. "I'm just messin'," he says.
   "'Ey there, Li'l Flow."

I give him a nod.
I don't wanna speak, but Uncle Reggie ain't havin' that.

     "Hey, Mr. Pete."

I head straight to my uncle's office, where it's warm.
   I mostly just chill on my phone—
no homework, thank God;
   all that stuff with Mrs. Rashad was enough—
     and wait for Cas to roll through.

After an hour or so, Uncle Reggie's calling me to come
   watch them do something to some lady's radiator.

Like I care about any of that!

I pretend-watch them flush the radiator,

my frozen fingers playing games on my phone,
feet rocking back and forth to keep warm.

"You ain't cold, are you?" Magic jokes. "De'Kari over
here freezing, Reg!"

The new guy looks over at me when Magic says that,
    and I'm expecting him to clown me, too,
but when Uncle Reggie goes to answer the phone
    and Magic checks the radiator lady out, he squints
    his eyes and goes, "What's yo name?"

"Flow," I say.

"But he called you De'Kari."
"So?"
"So"—new guy steps closer—"you go to Brookside?"
I barely get my "yeah" out.

New guy grabs me up so fast, my phone
    clatters to the concrete.
I lose my breath for a second.

"You that punk kid who put his hands on my li'l cousin!
You like hittin' li'l girls?"

My heart stops. Mouth open, no words.
New guy's shaking me, cussing at me, and I just know he
'bout to hit me.

"Ty'ree! TY'REE!"

Magic or Pete, one of them is calling him,
yelling at him
    to stop, let me go.
    But he's like me, when I fought Ebony.
        His cousin, Ebony.

Can't stop.

He's an Ace. An Ace like Brandon and them said.

I slam against something.

Dang, that hurts!

And then I'm free of Ty'ree.

Now Uncle Reggie is the one yelling and pointing.
    And Cas?
When did Cas get here?

Their mouths are wide and angry, but I can barely hear
    their words.
It's like I'm underwater.

Ty'ree swings, Cas swings, everybody's connecting.

Uncle Reggie, Pete, Magic.

Everybody grabbing, pushing, cussing, threats.

And then,
    it's quiet.

EB

Ty'ree comes home late. He missed dinner and the
   family meeting
that Granny said was mandatory.
   His voice drifts upstairs and wakes me up.
I climb out my bed, move near the stairs,
hear Ty'ree say, "Yeah, I got fired, Granny."

And Granny saying everything and nothing.

Granny call on Jesus,
   Granny ask what is wrong with Ty'ree,
why can't he do right?

I take a step down, then another, and another.

Please, Granny, don't put him out! Don't put him out!

It's not in my mind—I say it out loud.
Both heads turn my way.

"Ty'ree, what happened to your face?" His cheek looks
like mine did, and his jacket is ripped.

"NothingI'mfine."

Ty'ree squishes the words together. He looks anything
but fine.

"You was fighting?" I ask.

"Ebony, go to bed!"

"Hell yeah, I was fighting!

Ty'ree's
Getting
Louder.

"Told you I would take care
of that punk boy!
His brother, too!"

My heart is racing. Ty'ree fought De'Kari? He fought
  De'Kari's brother?

Did they try to jump Ty'ree? Two against one?

Do I know De'Kari's brother? It's probably that guy who
picked him up after our fight.

I *knew* that stupid stuff with Mrs. Rashad
  was a waste of time.

I bet De'Kari planned this whole thing.

FLOW

Why do people know . . . ? Why do people always find out
when stuff goes down?

My phone buzzes. Bryce knows. Brandon knows.

My phone buzzes. Jay-Jay knows.

I put my cracked phone on silent, slip it in my pocket,
while I sit at the kitchen table watching Cas pace as he
  tells Ma what happened.

Uncle Reggie's stayin' over, but I guess he's talked out.
He had his words with us at the garage.

Ma keep askin' if Cas is an Ace, and Cas keeps sayin',
  "Nah, Ma!"

He was just talking to a girl, an Ace's girl,
  but he didn't know.

And now the Aces are mad.

    They ain't the only ones.

I don't tell Ma how the Ty'ree guy threatened Cas;
she's mad enough that he put his hands on me.

"I'm pressin' charges!" Ma keeps sayin', and every time
she grabs her phone, Cas goes,
  "Nah, Ma, I'ma take care of it."

"Nobody wants *you* taking care of anything!"

Cas and Ma, voices loud, and I try to understand the
  mess . . .
and why everyone is out for us.

I bet Ebony told her cousin, the Ace,
  to come at me and Cas.

So much for
    kindness
and
    respect.

MIDNIGHT

EB

I can't fall asleep. Keep seeing Ty'ree's face, Granny's face.

De'Kari and his brother jumped Ty'ree?

I swear, it's *on* tomorrow.

This time I might handle things myself.

> For Ty'ree.

FLOW

Can't sleep. No way I'm gonna let this slide.

She really had her cousin come after me?

And now Cas is mixed up in it.

My fan is on high but I'm still HOT.

Nah.
This can't slide.

MIDNIGHT, AGAIN

Flow got a fresh cut, sharp, crisp lines
   that match the slant of his eyes
that narrow soon as he climbs on the bus.
      Nobody better say NOTHING to me. . . .
      'Specially not her!

Bus driver (Mr. Little) says "Mornin'," gets a half nod
   in return,
which don't fly.
Off the bus, try it again **"Good morning, Mr. Little."**
through teeth that are clenched, like fists. . . .
Fists that make Mr. Little (bus driver) watch Flow
move to his seat like he does hundreds of times
but different this time . . . only bus driver (Mr. Little)
don't have time to find out why.

     Arms folded across chest, warm coat to keep ALL the
      heat inside,
  but still, gotta clench toes and fists to keep from shivering.

     Nobody better say NOTHING to me. . . .

Eb got hair cornrowed straight back,
　　beads attack each other
each time her head swings.
Friends say, **Don't worry, we got you. Can't believe**
　　they jumped yo' cousin.
　　　　Jumped yo' cousin. Jumped yo' cousin.

Homegirls again, like no time has passed.
　　Sit three to a seat
even though the bus monitor says,
　　Naw, one of y'all gotta move.
Nobody's movin'. Nobody moves. Those well-practiced
　　glares
stay in place.

Don't worry, we got you. *Eb hears the words, but really,*
what her girls gonna do? Are they even her girls?
She got somebody to have her back way better.
　　Just wait.
After school.
　　Just wait.

Can't believe don't believe we at school so fast when
　　any normal day the bus ride be lastin' forever and ever.

Spill out the bus, laughter, joking, yawns,
　　eyes watching, searching,
whispers, plans.

Eb spots
Flow spots

Eb

Fingers fly, middle ones.
No smiles today.

    Just wait! Just wait till after school!
makes for a long day.

No breakfast, not hungry. Anger is a snack that fills.

Mrs. Rashad has questions; she's attached to the
   grapevine.
     I'm good.
       We're fine.
Respect.
Kindness.

Yeah, right.

We just celebrated Dr. King, y'all.
  We can honor him best
by being like him.

Whatever, Mrs. Rashad.

Social studies, math, ELA, who cares?
  Science experiment for what?
We're already volcanoes.

Daggers and looks could kill for lunch,
Instigators fanning flames with their mouths.

Eb 'n' Flow
Eb 'n' Flow . . .
They hear the heat, but no, we ain't doin' it here.
Too much like déjà vu.

> **You gonna handle her after school?**
> *Bryce, Brandon, Jay-Jay,*
> *Three Kings ready to swing on a Queen.*
> **We got you, girl.**
> *Kianna, Precious, Angie,*
> *Three Queens ready to descend.*

Bell rings.

Can't believe don't believe school over so fast,
when every normal day be lastin' forever and ever.

Spill out the school, laughter, joking, yawns,
eyes watching, searching, whispers, plans.

> **There he is!**

> **Look, bro; there she go!**

Heart racing, can't think, can't hear, reach for what
you got in yo' jacket. . . .
> *What you stole off your sister's key chain.*
> *What you swiped from the hall closet. Looks real.*

> *This is real.*

Wait.

That car look familiar.... It's Cas.

That walk look familiar.... Ty'ree.

What they doing here?

This ain't about them....
It's about us....
Eb 'n' Flow ... right?

What is this even about?

Voices.

Cas
and
Ty'ree.

Words.

Wait, did he just say that?

Things movin' fast,
too fast.
Tension, rising action, climax....

Wait!

Don't reach inside!

Don't walk closer.

Don't point!

That's my cousin!

That's my brother!

Shots.

Screams.

Silence.

THE RETURN

FLOW

Nah. Cas can't be gone. My head is pounding.
   My heart is pounding.

The thought of Cas not being here wakes me up.

Tiptoe to the den, where Cas is still wrapped up
   in the quilt Nana made.

He's snoring, which I really don't hate anymore.

If he woke up and caught me standin' here,
   just staring at him,
he'd have me in a headlock in seconds.

So I tiptoe back to my bed.

I don't usually be remembering dreams and stuff
and I definitely don't be waking up with my face all wet,
but that's exactly what happens today.

I wipe my face, stare at my fan. I'm shivering now.

I get dressed even though it's early. Put on the shoes
even though they not perfect anymore.

I remember telling my dad my Christmas list,
    and these shoes were on it, the very very top of it.

My dad said, "Well, it don't hurt to ask!"

And he was right.
It didn't.

I look at the pictures I have of him on my phone.

Smilin'. Laughin'. Clownin'.

I go to my messages.

I hope Dad's wrong about the feeling he has, and right
about everything else.

EB

They always be talkin' 'bout Dr. King having a dream,
    but yo . . .
I just had one, too. . . .

On everything I love, that dream felt real.

Seeing Ty'ree on concrete

Is this, like, a sign?
One of them vision things?

I swallow hard, feel my T-shirt sticking to my chest.
I'm a sweaty, hot mess.

      Good thing it's early enough for a quick shower.

Granny gives me my phone at breakfast, which is
      grits and toast and eggs and bacon.

"Ebony, don't you go there showin' out today,"
she tells me.

"I won't, Granny," I say.
That dream is making me mean it.

That, and Jaren's hug. He's holdin' tight, cryin' cuz he
   got used to me being here all day.

"I'll be home soon, aight?" I tell him.

He nods, even though he got tears all over.

I don't like when he cries, 'specially when it's cuz of me.

I sit by myself on the bus. Kianna pretends
   she don't see me, but she do.
     Angie sits in the row to my left and waves.

"Hey, Eb," she says.
I say hey.

I turn on my phone and the *ding*s go off right away.

Message
　Message
　　Message
　　　Message
　　　Message

My fingers freeze over a message from De'Kari.
　I take a deep, figure-eight breath
that would make Mrs. Rashad happy.

If I open this message, and see some mess,
　my whole day gonna
go downhill.

If I delete it and don't even think about that boy,
　I might be okay.

Delete.

FLOW

"Good morning, Mr. Flood."
　　"Good morning, Mr. Little."

"Good to see you back."
　　"Thanks."

Mr. Little's daughter, Sherese, waves at me,
　like she wants me to sit with her.

I wave . . . but I sit by myself.
   Her dad's eyes be all up in the mirror,
and me and Cas got enough drama with girls
   right now.

Cas.

I checked him, like, five times this morning.

That dream has me trippin'!

I look at my phone.

No messages from Ebony.

I asked a simple question.

Did u tell ur cousin to come at me?

It don't hurt to ask. Right?

EB

Mama say I'm too nosy for my own good, and guess what?

I am.

I can't stop wonderin' what that boy texted me.

I saw him twice in the hall and once in science, but
he don't really look mad. No mean-mugs,
accidental bumps, or whisper-threats.

Angie keeps askin' if we still got beef,
 if I'm gonna do somethin'.
I tell her to chill. Her and Precious and Jonetta and Bri
 got itchy fingers,
ready to record and post another fight.

Nah. Not today.

I text Ty'ree, who been blowing me up.
 I tell him I'm good,
don't need him to ride by the school.

Nah. Not today.

FLOW

I sit far from Ebony and her friends at lunch.
 Sat far from her in science class, too.
Since she wanna ignore texts,
I don't have nothing to say to her.

I do text Cas a few times to make sure he's okay.
That death dream still got me shook, yo!

I get a bathroom pass during math—guess I missed a lot
 being gone ten days.
All this new stuff is making my brain hurt.

Two steps down the hall and guess who I see. . . .

EB

They still talkin' 'bout MLK in social studies,
   and we gotta write our own
"I Have a Dream" speech.

I write about my dream last night and how
   I don't want it to come true.

Ever.

My eyes kinda tear up when I think about Ty'ree
   being dead.

I ask Miz Gardner for a pass, leave her class fast.

I take deep breaths as I walk, even do that arm thing
Mrs. Rashad showed us.

But then somebody comes out Mr. Lawrence's class and
walks my way.

You GOT to be kidding me!

Me and my mouth! I said it out loud. . . .

"What?" says De'Kari. His voice echoes down the hall.

"I'm sayin', what are the odds?" I say,
pointing from me to him.

He shrugs. "You never answered my text."

"I didn't see it."

"Whatever."

"Look, De'Kari, I don't want no drama with you."

"Then why you tell your cousin to come at me?"

I don't really know what to say.
I kinda told Ty'ree De'Kari's name.
I kinda said he was runnin' his mouth
    and needed to get handled.

But that was a long time ago, and I was mad
    cuz he sent me those messages.

"I ain't know he was gonna do that."

De'Kari glares, shakes his head. Keeps on walking.

And I don't know why, but I don't want him to. . . .

FLOW

    "My bad.

        About your shoes."

Huh?

I turn around.
She's got her hand on her hip and her face in
    attitude mode.

This her apology?

She don't even know.

"My dad gave me these. He's overseas;
someplace I can't pronounce."

"Your daddy in the army or something?"

"Yeah."

"Mine, too. But he's in Texas. I'm going out there
this summer."

"Good."

"Ummm, excuse you?"

"Just kidding." (Kinda.)

"Mmmm-hmmm. So you not gonna apologize, too?"

"Nah."

"Ooooh, see—"

"Chill, chill!" I say, cuz this girl got mad loud. "You
gonna have us back in ISS!"

She looks at me, waiting. And I guess what comes out
my mouth next is true. "My bad about the fight."

EB 'N' FLOW

"What class you in?" asks Eb.

"Lawrence," says Flow.

"Ugh, I can't stand him!"

"I know, right?"

Flow keeps walking.
Eb keeps walking.

"Oh yeah! I got a question!" Eb yells down the hall.

A teacher opens his door and shushes her. She's used to
    being shushed. She ignores him.

Flow waits for the question. It better not be dumb.
It better not stir things up again.

"Why you want people callin' you Flow?"

Flow thinks. He could say a lot. He could say a little.
She don't gotta know all his business. . . .
But like his dad says, it doesn't hurt to ask.

Or answer.

"Cuz it fits," Flow says.

And it does.

Acknowledgments

I visited the Motown Museum in Detroit a few years ago, and the tour started with an informational video about the history of Motown. The scene with Marvin Gaye discussing his groundbreaking album *What's Going On* continues to stick with me. Marvin said what he felt: "God is writing this album. God is working through me." I feel the same about the book you're holding in your hands right now. Here's why. . . .

I began writing *Eb & Flow* on a Saturday, with the words: "I don't hit girls." Maybe it has something to do with the title, but the words just *flowed* out of me from there. And on that following Monday, when I went to work at my middle school, there was a fight between a girl and a boy. As I walked with the young man to the guidance office, he was visibly upset and emotional over what had happened. His words to me? "I don't even hit girls!" I stopped in my tracks, not fully believing I had just heard my words spoken by a young man experiencing what I had *just* written about. Usually art imitates life, but in this case I experienced the opposite. That moment was powerful confirmation this story needed to be told.

And so my biggest acknowledgment goes to God, for like Marvin Gaye, I believe He was writing this story with me. All praises to Him!

A big shout-out to my agent, Hannah, for reading and receiving this story with as much joy as I felt writing it, and to Phoebe and Elizabeth, who were open to me trying something "different." I also have to give a shout-out to Ron Koertge, who was my workshop leader in my first semester at Hamline University. Ron read my workshop piece and threw out a question I wasn't expecting: "Have you thought about writing this in verse?" Ron, I absolutely *never* thought about doing that! I inwardly laughed at the suggestion and I didn't try it for that story. But this? This I wrote in verse, and it was the most connected I ever felt to a piece of writing. Thank you, Ron!

To my children, including those of you who snuck and read parts of this story in my notebook BEFORE I was finished, I love you beyond imagination! I'm doing this because I love it, but also to show you the magnificent combination of faith, passion, hard work, and Mamba Mentality. Listen to yo' mama . . . I'm kinda smart. ☺

Thank you to all those in the field of education who are pouring into Ebs and Flows every day. The work is worth it; continue to plant the seed.

And finally, to all my readers: Look to your left and your right, y'all! You have a lot more in common with the person next to you than you think. Find out how!

About the Author

KELLY J. BAPTIST is the inaugural winner of the We Need Diverse Books short-story contest. Her story is featured in the WNDB anthology *Flying Lessons & Other Stories* and inspired her first full-length novel, *Isaiah Dunn Is My Hero,* and its sequel, *Isaiah Dunn Saves the Day.* Kelly is also the author of the picture book *The Electric Slide and Kai* and the middle-grade novel *The Swag Is in the Socks. Eb & Flow* is Kelly's first novel in verse and was inspired by her ponderings about what really happens when kids serve suspensions.

Kelly lives in southwest Michigan with her five amazing children.

kellyiswrite.com

INTRODUCING ISAIAH DUNN

He's a poet and also the hero in *The Beans and Rice Chronicles of Isaiah Dunn,* stories his dad wrote about the superhero version of Isaiah.

He's the man of the family now, taking care of his mama and sister, Charlie, even when he could use some superpowers of his own.

Isaiah proves that with superhero courage—and a few great sidekicks—you can take on even the toughest of odds.

Praise for *Isaiah Dunn Is My Hero*

A Black Caucus of the ALA Best of the Best Selection

A CBC Best of the Year Pick

A Cybils Award Nominee

A *Booklist* Best Book of the Year

★ "An uplifting, affirming story for every collection."
—*Booklist*, starred review

★ "Isaiah's optimism, drive, and loyalty to friends and family make him a hero to cheer for, and lend a feeling of hope to this exploration of difficult topics."　　　　　—*Publishers Weekly*, starred review

"Inventive and heartfelt."　　　　　—*The New York Times*

Praise for *Isaiah Dunn Saves the Day*

Isaiah's heroic adventures continue when he finds out it's not easy being a mentor!

"A portrait of a boy who has been through difficult things and has received the love and support he needs from his community, enabling him to thrive and help others around him who may also be struggling."
—*School Library Journal*

"Isaiah's voice rings true, and his conflicts will resonate with readers, as will his efforts to support those around him."　　　—*Kirkus Reviews*

MEET XAVIER MOON

He's happy being out of the spotlight . . . until his great-uncle Frankie Bell gifts him a pair of quirky socks and challenges him to swag out and speak up.

A story about heart, confidence, and standing on your own two feet.

Praise for *The Swag Is in the Socks*

Midland Authors Children's Fiction Award Winner (2021)

A Junior Library Guild Selection

2022 New York Public Library Vibrant Voices Reading List

★ "A warm but authentic picture of a middle schooler figuring out who he is and who he wants to be, and how the support of a strong community can help a kid find their individuality."

—*The Bulletin*, starred review

★ "Readers, no matter their age, will be able to relate to Xavier's struggle to find confidence and express his authentic self."

—*Booklist*, starred review

Favorites with Kelly J. Baptist

What is your favorite color?
Turquoise

Who is your favorite athlete?
Kobe Bryant

What is your favorite food?
Soul food

Who is your favorite poet?
Elizabeth Acevedo

What was your favorite middle-grade book when you were a child?
Everything by Mildred D. Taylor!